Samantha
Sheen.

1 Hamreview upton-on
seven

1

Enid Blyton's

HAPPY HOURS STORY BOOK

Enid Blyton's

HAPPY HOURS STORY BOOK

(Samantha)
(Sheen)

Printed in Great Britain by Purnell & Sons, Ltd.
Paulton (Somerset) and London

CONTENTS

A Ship and a Pair of Shoes

"SHALL I help you sail your ship?" said a voice behind Sam. He turned round to see who it was.

"Oh—you're the girl next door, aren't you?" he said. "We're staying at Seaside House, and you're staying at Beach House."

"Yes, I'm Susan, and we came yesterday and we're staying for two weeks," said the little girl.

"How funny. So are we," said Sam. "Isn't my ship a beauty? I have it on a string because I don't want it to go sailing out so far that I lose it. My Uncle Dan gave it to me, and it was very, very expensive."

"Could I hold it for a minute?" asked the little girl.

"Well, no—I don't think so. You might let it go," said Sam. "Besides, you've got shoes on, and you'd get wet if you came and paddled where I am."

"Oh, I can take off my shoes," said Susan, and she slipped them off at once. She left them on the sand and came paddling beside Sam.

"Now let me hold the string," she said. "I do like sailing ships, but somehow girls never have ships of their own."

So Sam let her hold the string. The ship pulled at it as the wind blew strongly, and Susan gave a squeal. "It feels lovely, pulling like that. Oh—oh, Sam, the string has slipped through my fingers, quick, get it!"

Sam groped in the water for the string, but it slid away from him. He followed it, but soon he was in such deep water that his shorts were wet. He stood up and saw his little ship bobbing far away.

"You horrid girl!" he said. "I *told* you you'd let it go. My lovely ship. Oh, I never want to speak to you again!"

The little girl tried to wade after the ship, but Sam pulled her back.

"Now don't be silly! You'll get soaked! You've been quite silly enough already without that. Come back."

Susan was crying now. She paddled back to shore, very upset, and went up the beach. She sat down beside her spade and pail, looking very miserable.

Sam was angry. Let her cry! She hadn't lost *her* ship, she had lost *his*. Horrid girl! Why had he let her hold the string? What would his mother say when he went back to Seaside House and told her? She wouldn't be at all pleased.

He went off by himself with his own spade and pail, and dug a very big castle. Susan began to build one too.

"What a silly little castle hers is," thought Sam, patting his down hard. "Girls don't know how to sail ships, and they don't know how to build castles either. I shall never speak to Susan again."

When it was time to go home to tea he took his spade and his pail and went up the beach. Susan wasn't by her castle. She was at the edge of the sea, looking for something.

"If she's looking for my ship, she won't find it!" thought Sam. "It's miles away by now. My goodness me—how the tide has come in! The beach looks much, much smaller!"

He went in and had his tea. Mother didn't say anything about his ship, and he didn't like to tell her. She really would be very cross, he knew.

After tea he went out on the beach again. Susan wasn't there —but very soon she came down all by herself, and goodness me, she was still crying! How silly girls were!

She came up to him. "Sam, you know I took off my shoes

and left them at the edge of the sea when I sailed your lovely ship—well, I forgot all about them, and when it was time to go home, I looked for them and they were gone. You haven't seen them, have you? My Mummy is so cross with me about them."

"No, I didn't see your shoes," said Sam, "And I'm rather glad you lost them, because you lost my ship!"

He turned away and went off by himself. Then he felt ashamed. How unkind! He turned and went back to Susan again.

"Susan. I'll help you to look for your shoes. Come to where the edge of the tide is. Perhaps the sea has brought them up the beach," he said.

"Oh, yes—it might have," said Susan, and together they went to look all along the edge of the sea, which was bringing up seaweed and bits of wood and old shells and all sorts of things, as it always did when it came in.

They turned over the seaweed and hunted for the shoes. "They're white sandals," said Susan. "I ought to have changed into sand-shoes, but I forgot. That's why Mummy was so cross, because I wasn't supposed to go on the beach in my nice sandals."

"Let's go on to the next beach," said Sam, at last. "We've

looked everywhere here, and hunted in every bit of rubbish that the sea has brought up with the tide."

So they climbed over the groyne and went on to the next beach. Here the sea had swept up an enormous pile of seaweed, and the two children had a great deal of it to turn over. And then Sam found a white shoe! He pounced on it.

"Is this one of yours, Susan?" he said. "It is? Well, let's look along here for the other. They won't be far apart."

"That looks like something white over there," said Susan, pointing, and they hurried to it, "Oh—it's a bit of white cloth—no it isn't—it's the sail of a ship. Sam, Sam—it's a whole ship almost buried in the seaweed. Is it yours?"

Sam took it out very, very carefully, and beamed all over his face. "Yes, it's my ship. And hardly damaged at all—and just LOOK what it was lying on, Susan! Your other shoe! Really, what a bit of luck!"

"Oh, yes, it *is* my other shoe," said Susan, in delight. "Mummy will be pleased. And oh, I'm *so* glad we've found your lovely ship, Sam. It *will* be all right, won't it, it *will* sail on the sea again?"

"Oh, yes," said Sam. "I expect it just turned on its side, and got washed in to shore. I say—I'm jolly glad I came and helped you look for your shoes. I'd never have found my ship if I hadn't. Somebody *else* would have found it!"

"How dreadful!" said Susan. "Well, please don't be cross with me any more—and I promise never to ask you if I can sail your ship again."

So now they are great friends—and you should see the castles they build and the shrimps they catch, and all the paddling they do together—but Susan will *not* sail Sam's ship even though he says she may, and I think she's quite right about that, don't you?

The Little Toy-Maker

GEORGE and Fanny were excited because Mummy had said they might go out for a picnic by themselves.

"If you cross over the road very carefully and go to the hill above the Long Field, you should be all right," said Mummy.

So they set off, George carrying the basket because he was the boy. In the basket were some egg sandwiches, two rosy apples, a small bar of chocolate, and two pieces of ginger cake. There was a bottle of lemonade as well, and George and Fanny kept thinking of the cool lemonade as they crossed the road, went through the Long Field and up the hill. They did feel so very thirsty!

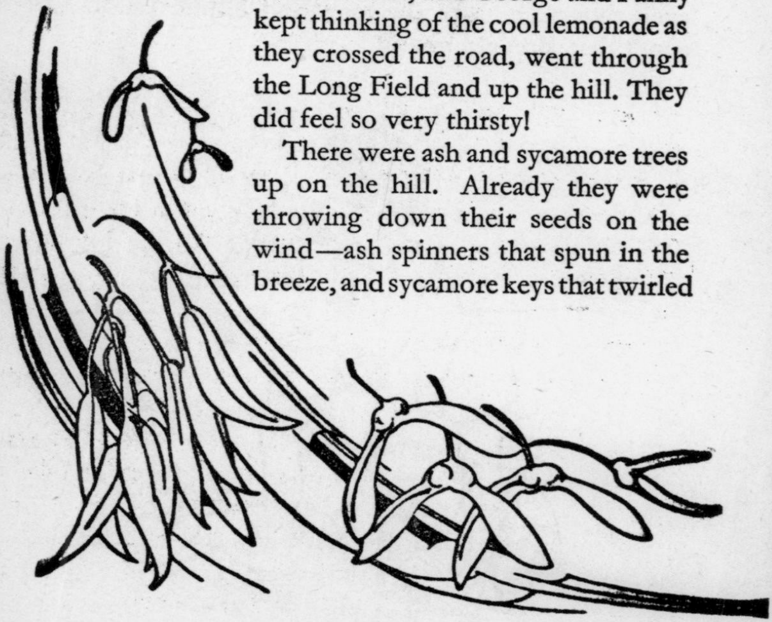

There were ash and sycamore trees up on the hill. Already they were throwing down their seeds on the wind—ash spinners that spun in the breeze, and sycamore keys that twirled

down to the ground. George picked some up and looked at them.

"Aren't they nice?" he said. "Throw some up into the air, Fanny, and see them spin in the wind to the ground. The tree is pleased to see them twirling in the wind, because then it knows that its seeds are travelling far away to grow into big new trees."

After a while the children sat down to have their lunch. They began on the egg sandwiches, but before they had taken more than a few bites they saw a most surprising sight. A very small man, not much higher than George's teddy-bear at home, came walking out from behind a gorse bush. He carried two baskets with him. Once was empty and one was full. The full one had sandwiches and milk in

it, and the children thought that the small man must be having a picnic, just as they were.

The little man didn't see them. He had a very long white beard that he had tied neatly round his waist to keep out of the way of his feet. He wore enormous glasses on his big nose, and he had funny pointed ears and a hat that had tiny bells on. The bells tinkled as he walked. Fanny wished and wished she had a hat like that.

"What a very little man!" said Fanny. "Do you suppose he is a pixie or a brownie?"

"Sh!" said George. "Don't talk. Let's watch."

So they watched. The little man walked along humming a song—and suddenly he tripped over a root, and down he went! His full basket tipped up, and out fell his sandwiches and milk. The bottle broke. The sandwiches split open and fell in bits on the grass.

"Oh! what a pity!" cried George, and ran to help at once. The little man was surprised to see him. George picked him up, brushed the grass off his clothes, and looked sadly at the milk and sandwiches.

"Your picnic is no use," he said. "Come and share ours. Do!"

The small man smiled and his face lighted up at once. He picked up his baskets and went to where the children had spread their picnic food. Soon he was sitting down chatting to them, sharing their sandwiches, cake, and chocolate. He was very pleased.

"Why was one of your baskets empty?" asked Fanny. "What were you going to put into it?"

"Ash and sycamore keys," said the small man. "There are plenty on this hill."

"Shall we help you to fill your basket?" said George. "We've eaten everything now, and Fanny and I would like to help you."

"Oh, do," said the small man. So the three of them picked up the ash and sycamore keys, and put them neatly into the basket.

"Why do you collect these?" asked Fanny. "I would so like to know. Do you burn them or something?"

"Oh no. I'm a toy-maker and I use them for keys for my clockwork toys," said the little man. "Come along home with me, if you like. I'll show you what I do."

He took them over the top of the hill and there, under a mossy curtain, was a tiny green door set in the side of the hill The little man pushed a sycamore key into the door and unlocked it. Inside was a tiny room, set with small furniture and a big work-table.

And on the table were all kinds of toys! They were made out of hazel-nut shells, acorns, chestnuts, pine-cones, and all sorts of things! The small man had cleverly made bodies and heads and legs and wings and there were the toys, very small, but very quaint and beautiful. The children stared at them in delight.

"Now, you see," said the little man, emptying out his basket of keys on to his work-table, "now, you see, all I need to do is to find keys to fit these toys, and then they can be wound up, and they will walk and run and dance. Just fit a few keys into the holes and see if you can wind up any of the toys."

In great excitement the two children fitted ash and sycamore keys into the toys, and George found one that fitted a pine-cone bird perfectly. He wound it up—and the bird danced and hopped, pecked and even flapped its funny wings. It was lovely to watch.

Soon all the quaint toys were dancing about on the table, and the children clapped their hands in joy. It was the funniest sight they had ever seen! They only had to fit a key to any of the toys, wind it up—and lo and behold, that toy came to life.

"I wish we hadn't got to go, but we must," said George at last. "Good-bye, little fellow. I do love your toys."

"Choose one each!" said the little man generously. So they did. Fanny chose the bird, and George chose a hedgehog made very cleverly out of a prickly chestnut-case and a piece of beech-mast. It ran just as a real hedgehog does when George wound it up.

And now those two quaint toys are on their nursery mantelpiece at home, and they are so funny to watch when George and Fanny wind them up with ash and sycamore keys. I can't show you the toys—but you can go and find ash and sycamore keys in the autumn for yourself if you like. There are plenty under the trees, spinning in the wind. Find a few, and see what good little keys they make for winding up fairy toys!

When Ellen Cleaned the Dolls' House

"WHAT shall I do today?" said Ellen. "I'm tired of all my toys, and I've read all my books!"

"Well then—what about giving your dolls' house a spring-clean?" said Mummy. "I had a look at it yesterday and really it is too dirty and untidy for words!"

"Oh yes—I could do that!" said Ellen. "Can I have a saucer of water, and a little cloth, Mummy?"

"Yes—and you can have this tiny little nail-brush to brush the carpets and scrub the floors," said Mummy. "It's such a nice dolls' house, and I'm sure the little dolls who live in it must feel very uncomfortable—everything is in such a muddle!"

Well, Ellen soon had a saucer of warm water with some soap powder in it. She had two little cloths, one for the windows and one for floors. Mummy gave her a tiny duster too, to polish the furniture.

It was certainly a pretty dolls' house from the outside. It had white-washed walls, a red roof, four chimneys, casement windows that opened—and a tiny garage at the side.

The whole front opened when Ellen wanted to play with the dolls' house. Even the lights switched on and off, and water came out of the taps from a small tank in the roof. Ellen could even fill the bath when she liked!

She began to spring-clean the house. She took down the curtains first. Then she took out the carpets and rugs. Then out came all the furniture, and soon the house was empty.

And then Ellen noticed a strange thing! The little dolls' house dolls weren't there!

"Where are they?" wondered Ellen. "There should be four of them, all tiny little things. I haven't seen them for a long time—but then I haven't played with my dolls' house for ages."

The toys who sat watching Ellen could have told her what had happened to the tiny dolls! The teddy bear had been a great friend of theirs, and they had told him how they hated living in a such a dirty, untidy little house.

"We'd clean it ourselves," they said, "but we haven't any cloths or brooms or dusters. We can hardly see out of the windows, they are so dirty!"

"Well, there's a lovely dolls' house in the toy-shop just down the road," the teddy bear told them. "There aren't any dolls in that. Why don't you slip out one night, and let me take you to the shop? Then you could live in that nice new dolls' house, and be sold with it, when somebody buys it!"

"That's a good idea," said the oldest doll, a pretty little thing in a blue silk frock. "We'll go tonight."

And so that night the bear had opened the front door of the dolls' house and called in softly, "Are you awake? I'm ready to take you!"

The dolls were awake. They all trooped out of the front door, and the oldest doll shut it quietly. "I'm not a bit sorry to leave!" she said. "Ellen never even comes near us, and hasn't played with us for weeks! Lead the way, Teddy, to our new home."

And off they went, out of the door, down the stairs, and through the kitchen door, which had been left open for the cat to come in. They soon arrived at the toy-shop, and the teddy bear lifted each tiny doll up to the letter-box on the front door, and slid her through it. It was lucky that the letter-box was so low down!

"Thank you!" the dolls called softly. "We can see the lovely dolls' house. It will be fine to live in a clean house. Perhaps a nice little girl will buy it one day and we'll all go and live with *her!*"

So that was why Ellen's dolls' house had no dolls living in it now! She simply couldn't *imagine* where they had gone to! She hunted for them everywhere, and the toys watched her, nudging one another.

"Wish we could tell her!" said the golliwog. "She would feel sorry she hadn't kept the dolls' house nice and clean then!"

"Sh!" said the bear. "She'll hear you! Now look—she's beginning to scrub the floors—about time too!"

It took Ellen the whole day to clean the dolls' house. She washed the curtains and Mummy ironed them. She cleaned the floors and the windows. She rubbed down the walls.

She brushed each little carpet and each rug, and washed three

that were very dirty indeed. Then she polished all the furniture —the little tables and chairs and cupboards, and the wardrobe that stood in the bedroom. She even polished the tiny bathroom taps, and put a very small towel on the rail there.

She filled the little tank in the roof with water, so that the taps would run properly.

"Now the bath can be filled too," she said. "But there isn't anyone to have a bath in it! Oh dear—WHERE can my dolls have gone?"

Mummy was very pleased when she saw the spotless little house. "Now your dolls will really *like* that!" she said. "Where are they?"

"I don't know," said Ellen. "They've disappeared! Do *you* know where they are, Mummy?"

"No, I don't," said Mummy. "They'll turn up somewhere, I expect. I'll have a look round."

But neither she nor Ellen could find the dolls! "You'll have to save up and buy one or two," said Mummy. "It's a pity that the dear little house shouldn't have anyone living in it!"

The toys thought so too. The big doll went to look through the windows, and said how lovely it looked inside. The bear peeped in too, and wished he was small enough to sleep in one of the little beds. "They look so cosy," he said. "I do wish we knew someone who would like this little house."

Then the golliwog remembered the pixie who lived in a hole in the apple tree, just outside the playroom window. He turned to the big doll in excitement.

"What about Tippitty the pixie?" he said. "She's always saying how cold she is at night, even though she has stuffed the hole in the tree with dead leaves. Do you think *she* would like to live in the dolls' house now that it is so lovely and clean? She's just the right size!"

"Oh *yes!*" said the bear, who liked Tippitty very much. "We'll ask her this very night."

So they tapped seven times on the window-pane, which was a signal for Tippitty to come and see them. She flew in at the top of the window, and landed just beside them.

"What do you want?" she said. "Oooh—I had to get out of my leafy bed—and it's *such* a cold night!"

"Come and see the dolls' house," said the bear. "It's clean and lovely now!"

Tippitty pressed her nose to one of the dolls' house windows and looked inside. The moon was shining brightly, and she could see everything clearly. It certainly did look very pretty and very cosy. "I'd like to go in at the front door," she said. "Oh, what a pity—whoever cleaned the house forgot to clean the little brass knocker!"

She went in at the front door and explored the whole house, while the big toys watched her through the windows. She could hardly believe it when water came out of a tap she turned on—and she loved the little mirror on the dressing table. "I've never had a looking-glass in my life!" she said. "Oh—I *do* wish I could live here!"

"Well, you can," said the big doll at once. "The dolls who once lived here have run away to the toy-shop, so the house is empty. You come, Tippitty. We'd love you to!"

"But—suppose Ellen peeps inside!" said Tippitty. "She might see me and catch me. I couldn't bear that!"

"You could easily hide in the big wardrobe in the bedroom," said the bear. "Oh do come, Tippitty. It would be fun to have you to play with each night. I'll keep the tank filled, so that you can have a bath whenever you want to. And when Ellen is out we could light a fire in the kitchen for you!"

"All right. I'd love to come," said Tippitty. "This very night! Shall I be able to sleep in this dear little bed—and wash myself in that little basin? I shall keep this house very, very clean and tidy if I live here!"

Well, she did go to live there and she is there still! She sleeps in the little bed, she has a bath when she wants to, and, when Ellen is out, the bear lights the little kitchen fire, and Tippitty sometimes bakes tiny fruit cakes for him!

And HOW tidy and clean she keeps the house! Ellen's mother is always so pleased when she looks in at the window to see it.

"Well, really, Ellen keeps her dolls' house beautifully

now!" she says. "What a pity no one lives in it. I do wonder where those little dolls went to!"

Ellen herself is very puzzled. One morning she looked in at the bedroom window of the dolls' house and saw that the little bed wasn't made!

And then she noticed that the tiny brass knocker on the front door was bright and shining!

"Good gracious! Surely nobody is *living* here!" she thought. "Is one of my dolls back—or is it a small mouse who likes a cosy bed? I must look into every little room and see."

So she looked in the kitchen and the sitting-room and the bathroom and the bedroom, and even the garage. But she didn't see anyone at all.

Tippitty was hiding in the wardrobe, of course, shivering with fright. Oh dear—would Ellen find her there and turn her out?

But Ellen didn't once think of looking in the wardrobe. So Tippitty is still living in the dolls' house, but now she is careful to make her bed as soon as she jumps out of it.

You'll know where to look for her if ever you go to tea with Ellen! Inside the wardrobe!

Dame Roundy's Stockings

DAME Roundy was a clever old woman. She made Lucky Stockings of red, green, yellow, purple, orange and brown. Whoever wore her Lucky Stockings would be sure to have good luck for a whole day. So you can guess that Dame Roundy sold plenty, and there were always elves, pixies, gnomes and goblins in and out of her front door, coming to buy her Lucky Stockings.

But she would never sell her Lucky Stockings to witches or wizards. "No," she would say, "I don't trust witches or wizards. They sometimes use bad magic instead of good. I don't want them to have my Lucky Stockings."

So the wizard who lived in Windy Wood nearby had to go without a pair of Lucky Stockings, although nearly everyone

else had them. He was called Wizard Shaggy because he had such big black eyebrows. He was not really a bad wizard, but he wasn't kind or generous as most of the people around were.

One day he badly wanted some Lucky Stockings. He had had weeks of bad luck, when everything had gone wrong that could go wrong. His chimney had smoked, and the sweep wouldn't come. He had fallen down and hurt both his knees badly. He had had a bad cold, and somehow or other he had made himself the wrong Sneezing-Spell, and instead of stopping his sneezing the spell had made him sneeze two hundred times without stopping, which was very tiring.

"I simply *must* get some good luck!" said the Shaggy Wizard to himself. "I shall go and ask Dame Roundy to sell me some Lucky Stockings—and, if she won't, I shall get them *somehow*!"

So he went to ask her. But she shook her head. "You know my rule, Shaggy," she said. "No Lucky Stockings for witches or wizards! So go away."

Now, that night Shaggy went quietly to Dame Roundy's and listened to see if she was asleep. She was. He could hear her snoring very gently, and he grinned to himself.

He knew where she kept her Lucky Stockings. She had a big red box, and into this she popped each Lucky Stocking as soon as she had finished knitting it.

Shaggy tried the kitchen window. It wasn't locked. He opened it very, very quietly. He climbed over the sill into the kitchen. He felt his way to the red box. He opened it and took out as many stockings as he could hold. He only wanted one pair—but he thought he could easily sell the others to wizards and witches, who were always longing for them and could never get them.

He shut the box. He climbed back into the garden. He shut the window. Then he rushed off to Windy Wood as fast as he

could go. Hurray! He had plenty of Lucky Stockings now, and he would soon get some good luck.

But when he got back to his cottage he began to feel rather uncomfortable. Suppose Dame Roundy guessed he had stolen them? She might send Burly, the village policeman, to search his house. Certainly he wouldn't dare to wear any of the stockings for some time in case people noticed that he had a new pair, and told Dame Roundy.

"I haven't been so clever as I thought," said Shaggy to himself. "I'll have to hide the stockings somewhere so that no one will know where they are!"

He looked at the pile of gay-coloured stockings, and scratched his head. Where should he hide them?

"I know!" he said suddenly. "I'll go and hang them up in the trees! Their leaves are all colours now—red, and

brown, and yellow and orange—and the gay stockings will match them beautifully. No one will guess they are hanging up in the trees among the bright autumn leaves!"

So out went Shaggy to do what he had planned. Soon all the gay stockings were carefully hidden among the leafy branches of the nearby trees. Then Shaggy went to bed, feeling quite certain that nobody would guess his secret.

In the morning Dame Roundy was amazed and angry to find her stockings stolen. She at once sent for Burly, the policeman.

"Shaggy the Wizard came to ask for some of my Lucky Stockings yesterday," said Dame Roundy. "I think you had better go and ask him a few questions, Burly."

So off went Burly to see Wizard Shaggy—and on the way what did he find but a yellow Lucky Stocking, dropped on the path that led to Shaggy's cottage! Then Burly felt quite certain that Shaggy had taken those stockings and had hidden them away.

Shaggy pretended to be very surprised to see Burly, and he told him a lot of naughty stories.

"No, I didn't take the stockings. No, I shouldn't dream of doing such a thing! No, I wasn't out last night, I was fast asleep all night through. I certainly haven't hidden the stockings. You just hunt around my cottage and see if you can find a single one!"

Burly did hunt, but of course he couldn't find any of the stockings. He looked in the shed outside. He looked down the well. In fact, he looked everywhere, even up the chimney, but he couldn't see a sign of those Lucky Stockings.

And yet he felt quite certain that Shaggy had them. Still, he had to go home at last, and Shaggy grinned like anything to see the back of him!

"Nobody will ever find out my clever hiding-place!" he said.

But that night a frost came. It was a very hard frost, and it loosened all the autumn leaves on the trees. In the morning the wind got up and blew hard. The leaves, which had been made very loose by the frost, began to flutter down in the wind.

Down came the leaves and down and down. Soon they

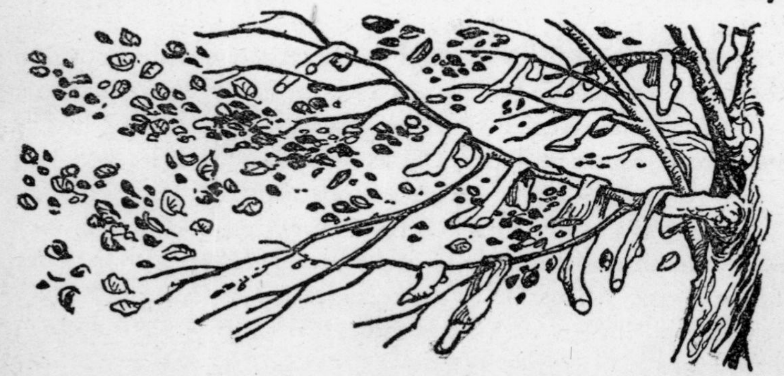

were ankle-deep in the wood. A crowd of pixies, coming home from school, shuffled through the leaves happily.

"The trees are almost bare," said one, looking up. Then he stared hard. "I say—what are those things in that tree up there! And look, there are some more over there—in that bare chestnut tree! And some more in that hazel tree! Are they funny long leaves?"

Everyone stared. "They look like stockings!" said another pixie.

"They *are* stockings!" said a third. "Dame Roundy's stockings—the ones that were stolen. They've been hidden in the trees. Quick, quick, come and tell Burly and Dame Roundy."

The pixies rushed off, and soon came back with Burly and Dame Roundy. While the pixies had been gone, Shaggy had suddenly noticed that all the leaves had fallen off the trees, and that the hidden stockings were now flapping and waving wildly in the strong wind. Anyone could see them!

In a great fright he rushed out and began to get the stockings down—and, just as he was doing that, up came Dame Roundy, and Burly the policeman!

"So you *were* the thief, and you *did* hide the stockings!" cried Burly, getting hold of Shaggy and shaking him till his hat flew off. "Well, you can just come along with me now. I've got a few things to say to you!"

"Oh, I thought I was so clever, hiding the stockings among the bright leaves!" wailed Shaggy.

"I suppose you forgot that leaves fall off in the autumn!" said Dame Roundy, collecting all her stockings. "Well, for a wizard, I must say you are really very stupid. Even a five-year-old child could have told you that!"

"What punishment shall we give him?" cried Burly.

"Let him come to me and learn to knit Lucky Stockings!" said Dame Roundy, with a smile. "It will be a good lesson for him to knit Lucky Stockings for other people and never be allowed to wear any himself!"

So that is what Shaggy *is* doing now—and he *does* have to work hard. Dame Roundy sees to that. If *you* want a pair of Lucky Stockings, you'll know where to go, but you have to be a good, kind person or Dame Roundy won't sell you any.

"We'll Stay Up All Night!"

"THERE!" said Granny, shutting up the book she had been reading to the twins. "There—the story's finished, and it's five minutes after your bedtime!"

"We'd like another story," said Peter. "We don't feel a bit sleepy, Granny! Read us a story out of *this* book!" and he put a big book on Granny's lap.

"No. To bed you go!" said Granny. "Really, I never knew such children for putting off bedtime! You're late every single night—I don't know what your mother would say if she knew!"

Peter and Pamela were staying with their Granny and Granpa and having a lovely time. Granny was kind and Granpa was fun. But bedtime was just as much of a nuisance when it came as it was at home!

"*I* should like to stay up till *you* go to bed, Granny," said Pamela.

"*I* should like to stay up all night," said Peter. "Not go to bed at all! What a lovely long time we should have for playing then."

"You'd soon get tired of it," said Granny, getting up. "Now go and turn on the bath water, Peter."

In half an hour's time they were in bed.

Granny kissed them both good-night and tucked them in comfortably.

"Where's Granpa—isn't he going to say good-night?" asked Pamela.

"He's not in yet," said Granny. "He'll pop in when you're asleep and have a look at you both. Now—no more talking!"

She left them each in their small beds, turned out the light and went downstairs.

It was a hot night and the twins tossed and turned, trying to find a cool place. They fell asleep at last—but woke up again later on, feeling so hot that they threw off their blankets and lay in just the sheets.

"Are you awake, Pam?" asked Peter. "Isn't it hot! I wish I had a bit of ice to suck!"

"Let's creep downstairs and get a bit out of the fridge," said Pam. "Granny and Granpa will both be in bed, because it must be awfully late now. They won't hear us if we're very quiet."

"Oh yes, let's—but we mustn't slam the fridge door too loudly," said Peter. "It would wake up Granny at once. Oh for a bit of ice—*two* bits! Come on, Pam."

They crept downstairs, Peter in pyjamas, and Pam in her nightdress. It really was much too hot to put on dressing-gowns. They went into the dark kitchen and switched on the light. It wasn't long before they had four bits of ice in a cup. They shut the fridge door as quietly as they could, but it was so heavy that they couldn't help making a noise. They stood and listened. Had Granny or Granpa heard? Would they come downstairs and catch them?

No—there wasn't a sound from upstairs. Good! "Let's go into the sitting-room and find a book to look at while we're having the ice," said Peter. So they went there and took two books from the book-shelf. They sat down and popped a piece of ice into their mouths.

"Oooh—it's almost *too* cold!" said Pam, and took hers out again. "I say, Peter, isn't this fun? Everyone's in bed, we're the only ones up. I'm not at all sleepy, are you?"

"Not a bit," said Peter. "I tell you, I could

easily stay up all night. It's silly to waste so much time in bed!"

"Well—why *don't* we stay up?" said Pam. "*I* don't feel sleepy either. I'm *wide* awake! I'd like to go on with our big jigsaw. And I'd like to play with our clockwork train set."

"No. That would make a noise," said Peter. "But I don't see why we shouldn't go on with the jigsaw. Granny would be awfully surprised if she saw it finished in the morning!"

"She might let us stay up later each night if she knew we'd been up all night long and loved it," said Pam. "Even an hour later would be *some*thing. Yes, we'll stay up *all night*, and we'll finish the jigsaw, and we'll read a whole book together, and . . ."

"Well, let's do the jigsaw first," said Peter, and went to the table where it had been left only half-finished, for it was a very big one. The twins set to work on it, sucking their bits of ice, which were now very small. It was difficult to find pieces that would fit without Granny to help.

After half an hour Pam yawned. "Why don't we do something else now?" she said. "We can go on with this later.

Let's get out all your little cars and build roads for them with bricks. I'll build the road and you build a garage."

But somehow playing games in the very middle of the night wasn't so exciting as in the daytime. For one thing Pam kept yawning, and that made Peter yawn too.

"We sound as if we're sleepy, but *I'm* not," said Peter, determined to stay up all night. "All the same, I think I'll have a rest from building. This garage is rather difficult. You will keep using the bricks I'm looking for!"

He leaned back against an arm-chair. Pam leaned against the couch nearby. "I'll have a little rest as well," she said—and will you believe it, in half a minute the twins were fast asleep! There they were, lolling back, their eyes fast shut.

Peter didn't know how long he had been asleep when he awoke, very suddenly. Some noise had disturbed him. At first he couldn't imagine where he was. Then he remembered. Of course—he and Pam were staying up all night! He put out his hand to awake Pam—and then stopped to listen. What was that noise? He listened intently.

Was it Granny or Granpa coming downstairs to find them? No—it wasn't footsteps coming down the stairs, it was someone opening the front door! He shook Pam sharply by the shoulder and spoke to her.

"Pam!" he whispered. "Wake up! Someone's trying to open the front door! It must be a burglar. Quick, wake up!"

Pam woke up in a fright and clutched hold of Peter. They both listened. Yes—someone had opened the front door—they heard the familiar cree-ee-eak it made. Then it was shut, very quietly, and someone began to tiptoe along the hall. Oh dear—what were they to do? Suppose the burglar came into the sitting-room and saw them? Suppose he took all Granny's silver ornaments that she was so proud of? Suppose . . .

"We'll hide, Pam," whispered Peter. "Quick—behind the couch!" So they crept behind the couch at once.

"He's gone into the kitchen," whispered Pam. "I can hear him opening the larder door. He must be hungry. Have we time to rush upstairs and wake Granpa?"

"Yes," said Peter. But just as they were creeping out from

behind the couch they heard footsteps again, coming from the kitchen into the hall, and they stayed where they were, holding their breath, quite still.

To their horror the sitting-room door opened and they heard a grunt. Then the light was switched off and the key was turned in the lock!

"The burglar's locked us in!" whispered Pam, very scared. "Whatever shall we do? Hadn't we better open the window and yell? Perhaps a policeman might hear us!"

"Good idea!" said Peter, and scrambled out of his hiding-place at once. He went to the window and opened it. "Help!" We've got a burglar here! Help!"

And then—what a wonderful thing!—a torch was suddenly switched on out in the road and a gruff voice said, "What's all this? Who's shouting?"

And it was the policeman they knew so well, who often held up the traffic in the town to let them cross the road!

"Oh, it's us, the twins!" shouted Peter. "There's a burglar in our house. He's gone upstairs! He'll frighten our Granny and Granpa!"

Well, quite a lot of things happened after that! The policeman got in at the window and was annoyed to find the door locked so that he couldn't go upstairs. Then Granny began calling out, and Granpa came running downstairs.

"What's up? What's the matter?" he shouted. "What's all the noise about?"

"We're in here! Unlock the door, Granpa!" cried Peter. "The burglar locked us in!"

The door was unlocked and Granpa came in. To the twins' surprise he was fully dressed! They had expected him to be in his pyjamas.

"Good evening, sir," said the policeman. "I was coming down the road when I heard these children yelling for help.

They say they heard a burglar breaking in at the front door, and then going to the larder, and then up the stairs."

"A *burglar*!" said Granpa, astonished. "What burglar? Why—I've only just come home myself, Constable—not more than five minutes ago! I was at a meeting! I went to the larder to get myself a slab of cake, and then went upstairs to bed. What in the *world* is all the fuss about? There's no burglar here!"

"Oh—a silly joke on the children's part, I suppose!" said the policeman, looking crossly at the twins. "Calling me in through the window for nothing. But they were certainly locked in here, sir."

"Well, I locked the door myself," said Granpa. "I saw there was a light left on, as I thought, and I switched it off and locked the door. I usually do. Whatever are you twins doing here so late at night?"

"Er—well—we were staying up all night long," said Peter, feeling very silly indeed now. "We *had* gone to bed—but we got up again. We thought it would be fun to stay up all night just for once."

"And—and we fell asleep, Granpa, and didn't know you hadn't come home," said Pam, beginning to cry. "So when Peter woke up and heard someone at the front door he didn't guess it was *you*, he thought it was a burglar. We were very frightened when you switched off the light and locked us in here!"

Granpa began to laugh. "So you called in the police, did you! Hallo—here's Granny. We've wakened her up—and I was trying to be so quiet and not wake her!"

Then Granny had to be told all that had happened, and she wasn't a bit cross. She began to laugh. "You silly, ridiculous children!" she said. "Apologize to the policeman and come up to bed AT ONCE!"

And so the twins went up to bed and immediately fell fast asleep. They were very very tired.

Will you believe it, at bedtime the next night Granny shut the book she had been reading to them and said: "Well, dears, now what do you want to do tonight? Go to bed as usual—or stay up all night?"

You can guess what the twins said, can't you? Stay up all night? No thank you—never again!

Hallo, Man in the Moon!

Once upon a time a little boy flew a kite in a very strong wind. The string broke, and the kite flew up into the sky, up and up and up.

"I shall go to the moon!" cried the kite. But he didn't. He flew on for a few hours in the wind, and then he dropped gently down to earth.

He was a fine kite. He had a big, smiling face painted on him, and he had a long tail of twisted papers. The little boy was sad to lose him.

He dropped down into the middle of a bramble bush, and the prickles caught him and held him. He stayed there, smiling away, and his tail shook a little.

Now a sandy rabbit lived under that bramble bush. He was sitting washing his ears when the kite fell down with a rustling noise.

"What's that?" he said to himself, and flicked his ears straight up to listen. He peeped upwards, and to his enormous surprise he saw a big face smiling down at him. It was the face that was painted on the kite, but the sandy rabbit didn't know that. He got such a shock. He sat and stared at the kite, and didn't know whether to smile back or not.

"Who can it be?" he wondered. "He fell down out of the sky. I think it must be the man in the moon! Yes, that's who it is—the man in the moon. He has come to live with me in my bramble bush. He must think I am a very important person indeed. Well, well, well—to think that the man in the moon himself should have come to live with me."

He smiled back at the smiling kite. "How do-you-do, man in the moon?" he said. "I'm pleased to see you. I will go and tell my friends about you, and see if I can get a few things to make you comfortable, if you want to live with me."

The kite smiled away, and the sandy rabbit hopped off. He went to the pixie who lived in the old oak tree.

"Dear Pixie," he said, "the man in the moon has come to live with me. Think of that! I want to make him comfortable, so will you lend me a chair for him to sit on?"

"Well, fancy the man in the moon coming to live with you!" said the pixie, astonished. "Yes—take one of my chairs. I haven't any cushions, but you could ask the blue goblin for one. He's got plenty. I'll carry the chair for you."

The pixie carried a nice little armchair. He and the sandy rabbit went to see the blue goblin, who lived under a gorse bush. He was blue all over, and a very kind person.

"Blue Goblin," said the sandy rabbit, in rather an important

voice, "the man in the moon has come to live with me. Think of that! I want to make him comfortable, so will you lend me a cushion for the pixie's chair?"

"Well, fancy the man in the moon coming to live with you!" said the blue goblin, astonished. "Yes—take one of my cushions. Don't you think you ought to borrow a big teapot, too? I am sure the man in the moon drinks tea."

"Yes, I think I'd better," said the sandy rabbit. "I'll go to the nobbly gnome and ask him for his teapot. It's a very, very big one. I do feel important. It isn't often the man in moon visits anyone, you know."

The sandy rabbit swelled himself up with importance.

Nothing so exciting had ever happened to him in his life before.

The pixie and the goblin went with the sandy rabbit to the nobbly gnome's house, which was under a hedge. The nobbly gnome was very bony and nobbly, but he had a nice face.

"Nobbly Gnome," said the sandy rabbit, in an important voice, "the man in the moon has come to live with me. Think of that! I want to make him comfortable, so will you lend me your big teapot?"

"Well, fancy the man in the moon coming to live with you!" said the nobbly gnome, astonished. "Yes—take my big teapot. And go to Mother Flip's and ask her if she will

spare one of her currant cakes. I know she has made some to-day, because I smelt them baking."

The nobbly gnome, the pixie, the goblin and the sandy rabbit all went to Mother Flip's. She lived in a very small cottage indeed, which had only one room.

"Mother Flip," said the sandy rabbit, looking more important than ever, "the man in the moon has come to live with me. Think of that! I want to make him comfortable, so will you give me one of your nice, new, currant cakes?"

"Well, fancy the man in the moon coming to live with you," said Mother Flip, astonished. "Yes—take my biggest currant cake. He will like it. I will carry it for you."

So all five of them went back to the bramble bush, carrying the chair, the cushion, the big teapot and the lovely currant cake. The kite was still there, smiling away.

"There's the man in the moon!" whispered the sandy rabbit, swelling up with importance again. "Isn't he nice and smiley?"

The others gazed at him. He wasn't really what they had expected to see at all. "Here's a chair for you, man in the moon," said the pixie, in a loud voice.

"Here's a cushion for you!" said the blue goblin.

"Here's a big teapot to make you plenty of tea," said the nobbly gnome.

"And here's a currant cake for you!" said Mother Flip.

The man in the moon just went on smiling. He didn't sit down in the chair. He didn't take the cushion. He didn't seem

pleased with the teapot. And he didn't even seem to want a piece of currant cake. He just went on smiling.

"Can't he do anything but smile?" asked the pixie, disappointed.

"Sh! There's someone coming through the wood!" suddenly whispered the goblin. They all crouched down in the bramble bush and hid. They could hear someone whistling. Then a boy came by.

He suddenly saw the kite caught in the bramble bush, and he gave a whistle of surprise and delight. "Wheeeeee-ew! Look at that! Somebody has lost his kite, and it's dropped in the wood! I'll get it, and if I don't hear of anyone who's lost it I can keep it and fly it."

The boy bent back the prickly bramble sprays and took out the kite.

He put it under his arm and went off, whistling. The kite still smiled. The sandy rabbit peeped out and saw it, as the boy walked away.

"He's taken my man in the moon who came to live with me," he wailed. "He's taken him away. He was such a nice man in the moon."

"I heard that boy say that it was only a kite," said the pixie.

"It wasn't, it wasn't! I tell you it was the man in the moon," wept the rabbit, and big tears ran down his nose and on to his whiskers.

The others were sorry for him. "Let's pretend it *was* the man in the moon," whispered Mother Flip to the others. "He's only a baby rabbit, really. He's very miserable, poor little thing."

"My man in the moon has gone!" sobbed the sandy rabbit.

"Sandy Rabbit, don't cry any more, because your tears are making a puddle under the bush, and we shall all get wet feet," said the goblin. "Now listen—you sit in the chair for a little while—and have my cushion at your back—and I will make a big pot of tea in the nobbly gnome's teapot—and we will all have a cup of tea and a piece of cake. Then we shan't mind about the man in the moon nearly so much!"

So the sandy rabbit sat in the chair with the cushion at his back, and they all drank cups of tea and ate large slices of

Mother Flip's delicious currant cake. The sandy rabbit felt important all over again.

"Anyway, the man in the moon *did* come to live with me!" he said. "I saw him fall down from the sky, I really did. And he smiled at me so nicely."

"Of course he did," said the pixie, the blue goblin, the nobbly gnome and Mother Flip. "Who could help smiling at a dear, funny little sandy rabbit like you!"

"Perhaps he will come to see me again," said the sandy rabbit, cheering up and taking another big slice of cake.

But I'm afraid he won't. Things like that don't happen twice, do they?

A Surprise for Goldie

It was the teddy bear's birthday. He was four years old that day, and he was very proud that he had a birthday.

"I didn't know about it till Janie told me," he said. "She came to the toy cupboard this morning and pulled me out and said, 'I must play with you specially today, Teddy, because it's exactly four years since I bought you. It's your birthday!' "

"What's a birthday?" said the clockwork mouse, who knew hardly anything.

"It's a day when people give you presents and make a fuss of you, and you have a cake and play with balloons," said the bear, remembering what had happened at Janie's own birthday party.

"Oh—well, we could give you a few presents, but they won't be new ones," said the big doll. "I'm afraid you can't have a cake, because the dolls' house stove doesn't cook properly. And there's only one balloon, and that's not blown up. It's at the back of the toy cupboard."

The golliwog gave the bear a present of a bead he had once found, and the sailor doll gave him a marble, and the big doll gave him an old brooch. He felt very rich indeed!

"Tonight we'll get the balloon out of the toy cupboard and blow it up," said the big doll. "We can bump it about like children do when they have a *real* party." So that night, when everyone had gone to bed, and only the toys were awake, they looked for the balloon. Yes, there it was, at the back of the cupboard—a flat, blue bit of rubber.

"How do you make it into a balloon?" asked the bear.

"Like this," said the doll, and she put her mouth to the neck of the bit of rubber. She blew hard, and the balloon began to swell. She blew again and it swelled a little more.

"You haven't enough blow," said the golliwog and he took a turn. He blew the balloon up very big indeed, and the teddy bear was pleased.

"Let's play football with it!" he said.

They really had great fun with the blue balloon. The goldfish swimming in its round bowl watched everything that went

on. It always liked night-time when the toys played games together, and was very excited whenever the little toy train raced by at top speed.

"Goldie's watching us," said the bear, pleased, and he gave the balloon such a kick that it floated high into the air and came to rest on the little table where Goldie swam in his bowl. Goldie was rather frightened when he saw the big blue thing. The bear climbed up to get it. He caught hold of it and pressed it to him—and oh dear, what a dreadful thing, the old brooch that the big doll had given him pricked the balloon—and, of course, it went POP!

It made such a big POP that Goldie was really terrified. He leapt right out of the water and landed with a bump on the floor. There he lay, gasping, waving his lovely tail helplessly.

"Oh! Goldie's leapt out! Quick, he will die if he isn't put into water!" cried the big doll. But nobody could lift him up on the table, he was too slippery and too heavy.

"Help, help!" he gasped. "I must have water!"

"What can we put him in, quick, think of something!" cried the teddy bear. "Is there a dish anywhere in the toy cupboard that we can fill with water for Goldie?"

The golliwog went to look. "No, there isn't," he said. "But there's a big doll's teapot that Janie uses when she gives us a party. Goldie could fit in there nicely, and have room to turn round."

"Bring it out!" shouted the bear. So the golliwog brought out the big round teapot and put it by the poor goldfish.

"Fill it with water from the puppy's water-bowl!" said the sailor doll. "Big Doll, help me to fetch it to the teapot. We'll tip it in."

So the big doll and the sailor carried the puppy's water-bowl to the teapot and tipped some of the water in. They spilt a few drops but that didn't matter.

"Now get hold of Goldie's tail, Big Doll—and I'll take his head," said the bear. "You hold his middle, Golly. That's right. Now—heave ho and into the teapot he goes!" And in went Goldie, and oh, how glad he was when he found that he was in water and could breathe again! He gasped and gasped—and then he began to open and shut his mouth more slowly—and at last, there he was, swimming round and round the teapot, with hardly room to turn!

"He'll be all right," said the bear. "Poor Goldie—we *are* sad to have to put you into a teapot, but it's the only thing we could think of!"

"Oh, that's all right," said Goldie, blowing bubbles in the water. "But please don't let anyone pour me out of the spout!"

"Oh—he must feel better, he's made a joke!" said the golliwog. "What a thing to happen on your birthday, Bear! It was that balloon that went off POP that made poor Goldie jump out of his bowl."

"Yes—and the brooch that the big doll gave me was what pricked the balloon," said the bear, taking off the brooch. "I think you'd better have it back, Big Doll, in case it pops any more balloons."

"There aren't any more to pop," said the big doll, but she took the brooch all the same, because she really did like it very much. After that they all played games, and the clockwork train took the bear for a special birthday ride round the room, sitting in the driver's cab. He felt very grand indeed.

But dear me, in the morning how surprised the children were when they saw a teapot full of water on the floor—and Goldie swimming round and round in it. They knelt down and stared as if they couldn't believe their eyes!

"We'll never, never know how Goldie left his bowl and came to swim in a teapot," said Janie. "Never, never! It's a Mystery!"

But you *will* know, if you read this story, Janie—and how surprised you'll be!

Oh, Flibberty-Gibberty!

Now once, on a lovely windy spring morning, little Flibberty-Gibberty felt full of glee. He leapt and he danced as he went through the primrose woods, and he shouted for joy. Then, just for fun, he pretended that something was after him. "I must run, I must run!" he shouted at the top of his voice. "The Big Blustery Breeze is after me! Ooooh!"

He leapt into the air as he ran, like a little mad thing. "Ooooh! It's after me! The Big Blowing Blustery Breeze is after me! It'll blow me to the moon! It'll sweep me to the stars! Make way, make way. I'm running for my life. Ooooh!"

The rabbits leapt out of his way in fright. A robin trilled after him, "Tirra-tatta, what's the matter?" But little Flibberty-Gibberty wouldn't stop.

A squirrel ran up a tree out of his way, and Flibberty-Gibberty raced by, his cloak blowing out like a sail. "Ooooh! Get out of my way! I shall be caught by the Big Blowing Blustery Breeze."

A little fawn jumped out of his way just in time, and stared after him with big startled eyes.

Why was Flibbery-Gibberty acting like this? Who was after him? The little fawn was frightened and raced after the pixie at top speed.

Then some rabbits ran after the fawn, afraid too. What was this Big Blowing Blustery Thing that Flibberty was shouting and leaping and dancing about?

The brownies smiled to see the mad little pixie go leaping. Whatever would he do next? One called after him.

"Flibberty-Gibberty, be careful of the Wandering Wizard. He's about this morning, and he's in a very bad temper. Don't you let him turn you into a toadstool and sit on you, as he did to Bron the Brownie!"

That made Flibberty-Gibberty slow down a little. The Wandering Wizard—oooh! He wasn't very nice. Nobody liked him much, but nobody could catch him, because he was much too clever.

But then Flibberty forgot about the wizard, and went flying through the woods as lightly as an autumn leaf, leaping and bounding as he went, still pretending to be scared to death!

And then, round a tree, who should he bump into and knock right over but the Wandering Wizard himself! My goodness me, what a thing to do! The Wizard went over like a wooden skittle and lay there, all his breath knocked out of him.

"Out of my way!" shouted Flibberty-Gibberty, not seeing who it was at first. "The Big Blowing Blustery Breeze is after me—oooh!"

"What's that?" cried the Wandering Wizard, clutching Flibberty by the ankle. "*Who's* coming? What's happening? My goodness, look at this fawn coming at top speed—and all these rabbits. WHAT'S HAPPENING, I SAY!"

"Let go my ankle! Run, run!" shouted the little pixie. "Run! I tell you the Big Blustering Blowing Breeze is coming! It'll blow you to the moon! It'll sweep you to the stars. Run!"

Just then the wind did blow, and very roughly too, so that the little clouds scudded across the sky like white rabbits. The wizard felt quite scared. He still held Flibberty's ankle and wouldn't let go.

"Help me up!" he said. "I don't know what to do. I'm

too old to run away. Oh, this wind—*I* don't want to be blown to the moon! Flibberty-Gibberty, help me up, I say!"

"Well, let go my ankle then," said Flibberty, quite fiercely. "I must run. I tell you, the Big Blowing Blustery Breeze is after me! Let me go!"

"You must help me first, before I let you go," said the Wizard, and stood up very carefully. He held Flibberty's arm now, and still wouldn't let him go.

"Whoooooooooosh!" said the wind, entering into the fun. It blew the Wizard's hat off, and Flibberty picked it up for him. The little pixie was frightened. Oh dear—he didn't want to be taken away by this Wandering Wizard! WHAT a pity he had bumped into him.

"Whoooooooooosh!" said the wind again, and tried to pull off the Wizard's flapping cloak.

"Take your fingers off me, you Blustery Breeze!" shouted the Wizard in fright. "Flibberty, what can I do? I'll be blown right away, for my big cloak will act like a sail!"

"Climb up into a tree!" shouted Flibberty, longing to get rid of the Wizard. "I'll help you!"

So he helped him up into a tree—and then the wind rushed down again in delight and shook the tree so that it bent from side to side and swayed like a ship!

"I shall be blown out!" shouted the Wizard. "And here comes the wind again! Flibberty, I shall be BLOWN OUT, I tell you. Think of something!"

"Give me your girdle and I'll tie you safely to the tree!" cried the pixie. "Ooooh—your hat might get blown to the moon. It will be waiting there for you when *you* arrive if I don't tie you up. Give me your girdle!"

So the Wizard undid his girdle with one hand, clinging to the swaying tree with the other—and Flibberty

tied him very, very tightly to the tree. Oh, very tightly indeed!

"You needn't be afraid of the Big Blowing Blustery Breeze now!" shouted the pixie. "If it blows all day and all night you'll be safe here, Wizard. Whooosh! here comes the wind again. Goodbye, goodbye—it's blowing me away again!"

And off he went once more, leaping, bounding just like the little fawn behind him, pretending to be dreadfully frightened. "Oooh! I shall be caught. Make way for me, I shall be caught!"

But he wasn't caught. Nor was the little fawn, nor were the skippity rabbits or the scampering squirrel. Only one person was caught and that was the Wandering Wizard tied so tightly to the tree. How he howled for help, as loudly as the wind! How he shook with rage, so that the tree swayed even more!

"Flibberty, come back! Untie me! Get me down! Flibberty, I'll turn you into a candle-flame and blow you out! I'll turn you into a lump of ice and melt you. I'll—I'll . . ."

But Flibberty-Gibberty was far away, tired out with all his leaping and jumping and pretending, fast asleep with the tired rabbits and squirrel and little fawn cuddled up to him. What a day! What a wonderful, blustery windy day!

"It was fun," said Flibberty in his dreams. "Oh, it was FUN!"

Betsy-May and the Bear

BETSY-MAY had a beautiful doll's pram. It was green and had a hood that went up and down like the hood on her baby-brother's pram. It had a brake too, and a shining handle. It was really lovely.

Betsy-May took her dolls and her bear out every single day in the pram. She said they liked an outing as much as Baby James.

"Teddy-bear likes it best of all," she told her mother. "He needs a lot of fesh air. He told me so."

"Did he really?" said her mother. "Well, he is a most sensible bear then. He knows what is best for bears and little girls too. You must take him out every day, Betsy-May."

Now one day something went wrong with Betsy-May's doll's pram. A big screw came out and Betsy-May didn't notice it. It fell on the ground. Then a wheel came loose because the screw wasn't there, and at last it came right off. Betsy-May was most upset.

"Now don't get worried," said Mummy. "We will take it to the bicycle-shop and leave it there to be mended. They will only take a little while to do it."

But the bicycle-man was very busy mending bicycles, and he said it would be two days before the pram was mended. Betsy-May was sorry.

"My dolls and my bear will miss going out for their walk," she told the man. "Can't you mend it to-day, please?"

"No, I can't, Missy," said the man. "Your dolls and your bear had better have a cold and stay in bed to-day and to-morrow. Then they won't mind not going out."

"They've only just *had* colds," said Betsy-May. "They can't have another one just yet. Well, never mind. They must be patient."

Betsy-May went to look at her dolls and her bear the next day. "I am very, very sorry not to be able to take you out," she said. "But the pram isn't mended yet. I do hope you won't mind very much."

The dolls looked up at her with smiling faces. But the bear didn't smile. Betsy-May looked at him. She thought he really looked very sad.

"Cheer up," she said. "It's only to-day and to-morrow you can't go out."

But the bear still looked very sad. Betsy-May quite expected to see tears running out of his eyes, but though she watched him for quite a long while, he was brave enough not to cry.

Betsy-May felt unhappy because her bear was unhappy. He came to bed with her every night, and he was her favourite

toy. He was so soft and cuddlesome, and he had such a nice friendly face. She went to nurse and told her.

"He looks dreadfully sad," she said. "I do wish I could borrow a pram from somewhere. I suppose you wouldn't let me have Baby's pram, would you? I'd be very careful."

"Good gracious, no!" said nurse. "If you so badly want to take your bear out, why don't you put a cushion in your little barrow, and a rug or two, and take the bear out in that?"

"That *is* a good idea!" said Betsy-May in delight. "I'll get it."

So she got the little barrow and made a nice bed inside it with a little pillow, a tiny mattress, a sheet, and a rug.

"What shall I do for a hood?" she wondered. "He must have a hood over him, because of the sun. He doesn't like the

sun in his eyes. Oh—I know! I'll get a little umbrella—my own one—and put it up for the hood."

So she did. Really, the barrow looked fine, almost like a pram!

Betsy-May set off with the barrow-pram. She went down the garden, and out of the gate at the bottom into the quiet little lane. She wheeled the barrow along for a good way and then she met Mrs. Jordans.

"Good morning, Betsy-May," said Mrs. Jordans. "That's a funny pram you have this morning! Which doll are you taking for a walk?"

"It's my teddy-bear I'm taking," said Betsy-May. "He's under the umbrella. That's for a hood, you see."

Mrs. Jordans peeped under the umbrella. Then she lifted it a little and peeped again.

"Well, that's funny," she said, "I can't see him!"

Betsy-May lifted up the umbrella in alarm. Goodness gracious, there was no bear there! How very astonishing!

"Where's he gone?" cried Betsy-May. "Oh, Mrs. Jordans, please help me to look for him! He's my own darling favourite bear, and he goes to bed with me at night. Oh, where can he be? Do you suppose he jumped out of the barrow because he didn't like it?"

"I shouldn't really think so," said Mrs. Jordans.

Betsy-May looked up and down the lane, hoping to see a small bear running away. But there wasn't one to be seen. She began to cry bitterly.

"Oh, he's gone! I've lost him! I only took him out in the barrow because he looked so sad. And now he's quite, quite lost."

Mrs. Jordans tried to comfort Betsy-May, but the little girl pushed away her hand and ran home, with the barrow bumping up and down in front of her. She ran up the garden, sobbing loudly. Nurse looked out of the nursery window, most alarmed.

"Betsy-May, have you hurt yourself?" she called. "What's the matter?"

Betsy-May rushed upstairs to nurse, still crying. "Oh, a dreadful thing has happened!" she wept. "I've lost Teddy. He's gone. He jumped out of my barrow."

Nurse looked at Betsy-May and laughed. "Then he must have run back home very quickly," she said. "Because there he is on that chair, Betsy-May."

Betsy-May looked at the chair—and sure enough, there was the teddy-bear sitting on the chair, with a little straw hat on his head, and a little scarf round his neck.

"Oh! The darling! He's here after all!" squealed Betsy-May, and she ran to the bear and took him up to hug him. "Oh, did you run all the way back? Oh, how glad I am to have you again!"

Betsy-May sat down on the chair with the bear and thought hard. She went very red.

"What's the matter now?" asked nurse.

"Do you know, I'm a very silly girl," said Betsy-May in a rather small voice. "I don't believe I put Teddy into the barrow at all. I arranged it all so beautifully for him and put the umbrella on top for a hood—and then I went off without him! I couldn't see he wasn't there, because of the umbrella. Do you think he thinks I'm very silly?"

"No, I should think he feels as I do—that you really are the funniest child in the world!" said nurse. "I should think he wants to laugh, just as I do!"

And when Betsy-May looked at the bear, he didn't look sad any more. He really did look as if he wanted to laugh! And I'm not surprised at that, are you?

The Little Blue Kitten

"WHAT'S that sitting on Dame Grumpy's windowsill across the road?" said Gobbo, looking out of his front door.

"Good gracious! It looks like a kitten—but it can't be, because it's as blue as the sky!" said his brother Winky.

"Let's go and see," said Gobbo, so they ran across and leaned over the wall. "Yes," said Gobbo, "it *is* a blue kitten. Well, I've never in my life seen a blue kitten before. Puss, Puss, Puss!"

Dame Grumpy looked out of the window at once. "Now, just you leave my kitten alone!" she said. "I know you two mischievous little goblins! If you dare to tease my blue kitten I'll rub spells on your noses and make them grow as long as cucumbers!"

"Oh no, please don't," said Gobbo, in alarm. "We're not mischievous, really we're not. You're thinking of our cousins Hoppy and Jumpy—they really *are* naughty. We only just

came to look at your blue kitten. I suppose you wouldn't let us play with it sometimes? We could give it an empty cotton-reel to roll about—it would love that."

"You leave my blue kitten alone!" said Dame Grumpy. "If I see you anywhere near it I'll come after you with my Spanking Slipper!"

"Meow!" said the kitten, looking at Gobbo and Winky.

"There! It's talking to us!" said Gobbo, very pleased. But Dame Grumpy picked it up and went indoors with it at once.

"We'd better be careful," said Gobbo. "I don't like that Spanking Slipper of hers. Let's go back."

Well, the two little goblins didn't go near the blue kitten. They just waved to it when they went out to do their shopping, but that was all. Then one day as they took their big round basket with them to shop at the market, they saw that the kitten wasn't on Dame Grumpy's windowsill as usual.

"It must be indoors," said Gobbo—and just at that minute Dame Grumpy came out, calling "Puss, Puss, Puss!" Then she saw the two goblins and frowned.

"Have you taken my kitten to play with? You know what I told you—I'll rub a spell on your noses and . . ."

"Please, Dame Grumpy, we haven't seen the kitten this morning," said Gobbo, in a hurry, backing away quickly. "We've never even stroked it, though we'd like to!"

"Well, if I see you with it, I'll spank you, just as I said," said Dame Grumpy. "Puss, Puss, Puss, where have you gone to? Oh dear—I do hope it hasn't run away!"

"Come on, let's go and do our shopping," said Gobbo. "My goodness—I'd certainly run away from Dame Grumpy if I was her kitten—wouldn't you, Winky?"

They went off down the road. They were soon at the market, and bought such a lot of things. Six rosy apples, six big brown eggs, a pound of butter, a round chocolate cake, and a pound of nice fat sausages. The basket was quite full by the time they had finished. They went off home again—and then, just as they passed under a big chestnut tree, they heard a sound that made them both stop at once.

"Meow! Meeee-ow! Meeeeeee-ow!"

"That's a cat mewing—and it's frightened!" said Winky at once. "Where is it? Puss, Puss, Puss!"

"Mee-ow-ee-ow-ee-ow!" said the cat, wherever it was.

"It sounds as if it's up this big tree," said Gobbo, and he looked up into the branches. "Yes—it is! And, Winky—it's the little blue kitten!"

"So it is!" said Winky, peering up too. "It must have

wandered away from Dame Grumpy's and climbed up this tree. Perhaps a dog frightened it."

"Come down, kitty!" called Gobbo. "Come along. We'll take care of you. You needn't be frightened of dogs."

"Meeeee-ow-owl!" said the kitten, sadly, and didn't move at all. It was much too frightened. The ground looked a long way away, and it was afraid of falling. It had never been up a tree before, and it didn't much like it now it was there.

"Little kittens shouldn't climb big trees," said Gobbo, looking up at it. "Winky, what can we do? We can't leave it there. It might never come down."

"Well, I'll climb up and see if I can get it," said Gobbo, and up he went. But as soon as he came near the kitten it climbed a little higher! But at last Gobbo managed to catch it and it snuggled into his arms.

"Oh good!" called Winky. "Come on down."

"I can't!" said Gobbo. "I want my arms to climb down with, but I can't use them because I'm holding the kitten. I shall fall if

I don't use my arms. Oh dear, don't wriggle so, kitten. Winky, what shall we do?"

"I don't know," said Winky, and he frowned. Then a good idea came into his head. "Gobbo!" he called, "shall I empty out all the things in our basket, and climb up the tree with it? We could put the kitten into it, and lower it down the tree."

"But what shall we lower it with?" said Gobbo.

"I'll pop into Ding-Dong's house, and ask him if he'll lend me his kite-string," said Winky. So he ran to Ding-Dong's house, and Ding-Dong said yes, certainly he could borrow his kite-string. So it wasn't long before Winky was back again. He emptied everything out of the basket and tied the string to the handle. Then he climbed up the tree with the basket.

"Here we are!" he said to Gobbo. "Now—put the kitten very carefully in the basket. I'll climb down, and you can let the basket swing down to the ground. I'll be there to take out the kitten." Well, they were *just* doing that when Gobbo gave a yell that almost made Winky fall out of the tree.

"Winky, quick! Look, there's that wicked little Hoppy down there—and Jumpy too—and they're picking up all our shopping. Quick, climb down and stop them!" Winky climbed down so fast that he almost lost his footing! But when he came to the bottom of the tree, Hoppy and Jumpy had gone—and so had the brown eggs, the rosy apples, the butter, the nice fat sausages and the round chocolate cake! Oh, those bad little goblins!

"Just wait till I see them!" said Winky, almost in tears. "Gobbo, swing the basket down now, gently, very gently. Oooh—careful! I do hope the kitten won't jump out!"

The kitten lay quietly as the basket swung down—and even when Winky caught it, the little thing didn't move. It seemed to like the basket, it gave a little purr, shut its eyes and went to sleep!

"Dear little kitten!" said Winky. "Oh dear—I'm glad to have rescued you, but you've made us lose all our shopping!"

Gobbo climbed down and the two goblins went off, carrying the sleeping kitten in the basket—and whom should they meet round the corner, but Dame Grumpy!

"Oh my goodness!" said Gobbo, and stopped. But it was too late—Dame Grumpy had seen the kitten in their basket.

"*You* had my kitten after all!" she cried. "You took it away in your basket! I'll put a spell on your noses to make them long as cucumbers! I'll get my spanking slipper, I'll . . ." But the goblins didn't wait to hear any more. They fled down the road, and into their house with the kitten—and slammed and locked the door! When Dame Grumpy came panting up, they called from their bedroom window.

"You shan't have your kitten back till you promise not to put a spell on us. It was up a tree and we rescued it! We emptied our shopping-basket and borrowed Ding-Dong's kite-string, and let it down in the empty basket—and while we were doing that Hoppy and Jumpy stole all our shopping."

"You get us back our shopping and you can have your kitten!" shouted Winky.

"Is this all true?" said Dame Grumpy. "Well, I'm very, very sorry I chased you. I'll make a spell straight away to bring back your shopping!" And hey presto, she waved her stick in the air and muttered some strange magic words.

Good gracious! What was this flying through the air? A string of sausages! Six brown eggs, followed by six rosy apples! A pound of butter and a round chocolate cake! They all came quietly to rest on the garden seat. Gobbo and Winky could hardly believe their eyes.

"Now come on down with my blue kitten," said Dame Grumpy. "You're very kind. I'm sorry I was so cross—but it isn't often that goblins are helpful, you know."

So Gobbo and Winky came down into the garden, carrying the sleeping kitten in the basket. It looked so sweet and comfortable. "We'll lend you the basket till it wakes up," said Winky. "Please—do you think we could come and play with it sometimes?"

"Of course. Whenever you like!" said Dame Grumpy. "But just let me warn you—keep indoors for the next ten minutes. I'm sending my Spanking Slipper after those two bad goblins, Hoppy and Jumpy!"

So Gobbo and Winky kept safely indoors—and goodness me, they saw that Spanking Slipper hopping along the road, looking for the goblins!

"There it goes, looking for Hoppy and Jumpy," said Gobbo, with a giggle. "My word—won't they get a shock when it hops into their kitchen!"

They will—but I don't feel a bit sorry for them, do you?

Well Really, Lazy Luke

ONCE upon a time Lazy Luke fell asleep in front of his fire, and when he woke up it had gone out. He shivered.

"Look at that now—the fire's out and I've no more wood. I'll go and borrow a bundle from Dame Hurry-About."

So he went across the road to Dame Hurry-About's cottage and asked her for some wood.

"You lazy fellow!" she said. "Why don't you go to the woods and pick some up—there's plenty there!"

"It's a long way," said Lazy Luke. "You just lend me a few sticks, Dame Hurry-About, and I'll bring you plenty tomorrow."

"Well, you do something for *me* first," said Dame Hurry-

About. "You go and ask Mr. Borrow-A-Lot to let me have back the teapot of mine I lent him yesterday. Then I'll let you have some sticks."

"Oh bother! He lives up the hill," said Lazy Luke.

"Well, no teapot, no sticks," said Dame Hurry-About, so Luke had to go. He walked up the hill to Mr. Borrow-A-Lot and saw him sitting down having a cup of tea out of Dame Hurry-About's teapot.

"Dame Hurry-About says, please will you give me her teapot that you borrowed yesterday," said Lazy Luke.

"Well, as you can see, I'm using it," said Mr. Borrow-A-Lot. "But I'll be finished in five minutes. You just pop down to Mother Cranky's and ask her if she can spare me a new-laid egg. She said she might have one for me today."

"Oh *dear*!" said Lazy Luke. "All that way! No, I'll sit down and wait till you're ready to give me the teapot."

"Oh no you won't," said Mr. Borrow-A-Lot. "No new-laid egg, no teapot!"

So Lazy Luke went off to Mother Cranky's, and he had to knock at her door four times before she opened it.

"Now, now, now, who's this waking me up out of my nap!" she said crossly. "Oh, it's you, Lazy Luke. What do you want?"

"Mr. Borrow-A-Lot says you promised him a new-laid egg today," said Lazy Luke. "I've come to get it for him."

"Well, fancy you putting yourself out to do a job for any-one!" said Mother Cranky. "That does surprise me! I'll have to go and look in my hen-house to see if there's an egg there. You do something for me while I'm looking. Pop over to Father Hoo-Ha's and ask him to let you have his ladder for me. I just want to borrow it till tomorrow, to clean the top shelves of my larder."

"But I don't want to have to carry a ladder all the way back here!" said Lazy Luke in horror!

"All right. No ladder, no new-laid egg," said Mother Cranky, and shut the door in his face.

"I'll fetch the ladder, I'll fetch it!" shouted Lazy Luke. "You get the egg!" And away he went again, grumbling loudly.

"Fetching and carrying like this! What do people think I am? An errand-boy?"

He came to Father Hoo-Ha's little house and knocked at the door. But Father Hoo-Ha wasn't indoors, he was right at the bottom of his garden. So Lazy Luke had to go round the back way and walk all the way down to him.

"And what's brought *you* so far from your fireside today?" said Father Hoo-Ha.

"Mother Cranky says, please will you lend her your ladder?" asked Lazy Luke.

"What! Do you mean to say you've offered to carry it to her?" said Father Hoo-Ha, astonished. "Wonders will never cease. Well, it's in my shed, so I'll have to get it out. You go round to Mr. Long-Whiskers while I'm getting it, and ask him to lend me his bicycle, please. He always lends it to me when I want it."

"Oh *no*," said Lazy Luke. "No, I can't do that! I can't ride a bicycle and I'm not going to walk all the way back here pushing one!"

"Well, then—no ladder," said Father Hoo-Ha, turning back to his gardening. "No bicycle, no ladder—see?"

Lazy Luke did see. He sighed. "I'll get the bicycle—but all I hope is that Mr. Long-Whiskers hasn't got a job *he* wants doing as well. I'm tired of doing jobs."

"Tired? You're always tired, you are, Lazy Luke!" said Father Hoo-Ha. "It's a wonder to me you ever get up in the morning, it really is. Well now, do go along, I shall have the ladder ready for you before you're back!"

Lazy Luke went off, groaning. His legs felt shaky and his head ached. Oh how tired he felt, doing so many things for so many people!

Mr. Long-Whiskers was baking cakes, and he wasn't very pleased to see Lazy Luke. "What do you want?" he said. "You're just in time to do a job for me. Look, my oven isn't hot enough. Will you just pop out to the wood behind my house and bring back some wood for it?"

"No, I won't," said Lazy Luke. "Good gracious, that's what *I* wanted for my own fire, and here I've come for miles and done all kinds of jobs so that I can borrow some from Dame Hurry-About! If I'd wanted to fetch wood I'd have done it for myself, not for you!"

Mr. Long-Whiskers picked up a broom and gave Lazy Luke a hard spank with it. "You do as you're told!" he said. "You haven't told me yet why you've come."

"Oh—to borrow your bicycle for Father Hoo-Ha," said Lazy Luke. "Please don't spank me again with that broom. I'll go and get the wood for you!"

And away he hurried to the wood, gathered a great armful

of dead wood, and hurried back. He did hope that Mr. Long-Whiskers had put that broom away!

He had—and he had got the bicycle out ready for Lazy Luke. "Oh, thanks," said Lazy Luke and wheeled it off at once. But he was so tired that he really felt as if he must ride it.

So he tried—and fell off at once. Goodness, what a crash he had! He bumped his head very badly indeed, and after that he decided to wheel the bicycle. He came to Father Hoo-Ha's and asked him for the ladder.

"Here's the bicycle," he said. "Oh my goodness—what an enormous ladder! Haven't you a smaller one?"

"No," said Father Hoo-Ha. "Ha—perhaps it will do your lazy bones good, carrying that all the way to Mother Cranky!"

Poor Lazy Luke. He staggered along to Mother Cranky's with the enormous ladder, and let it drop in her garden with a sigh of relief. He knocked at the kitchen door.

"I've brought the ladder," he said. "Can I have the egg?"

"Egg? What egg?" said Mother Cranky. "Bless us all, what do you mean?"

"You said you'd give me a new-laid egg for Mr. Borrow-A-Lot if I fetched that ladder," said Lazy Luke. "You did, you did!"

"Dear me, yes—I remember," said Mother Cranky. "You've been so long that I'd forgotten about it. Here it is."

Lazy Luke took it and went off to Mr. Borrow-A-Lot. Goodness, what miles he had walked! He looked at his shoes —just see, one of his toes was poking through his shoe! Now he would have to pay for it to be mended!

He came to Mr. Borrow-A-Lot's house and looked in at the window. Well, he was still having cups of tea out of Dame Hurry-About's teapot! Would you believe it! Lazy Luke was so cross that he walked straight in at the door without knocking.

"Manners, manners!" said Mr. Borrow-A-Lot. "You want the teapot, I suppose? You've been so long that I've brewed another pot. Have a cup?"

"*No,*" said Lazy Luke angrily, and put the new-laid egg down on the table. "You ought to have had it washed and ready for me."

"You can go and wash it yourself if you talk like that," said Mr. Borrow-A-Lot. "And by the way—could you lend me sixpence? I don't seem to have any sixpences left."

"Ho! Haven't you! How strange—neither have I, Mr. Borrow-A-Lot!" said Lazy Luke. He took the teapot and rinsed it angrily under the tap. Really, the things he had done

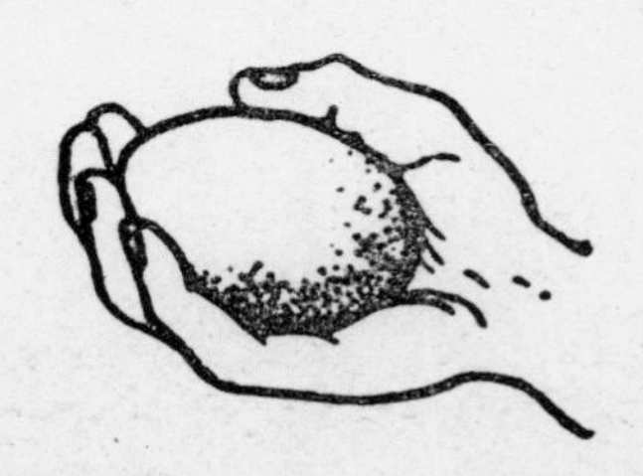

this afternoon! He would have made a fortune if everyone had paid him for his work! He took the teapot to Dame Hurry-About's, and, oh dear, what was this? There was a note on the door for Lazy Luke. This is what it said: "To Lazy Luke. I got tired of waiting for you. Leave my teapot on the doorstep. You can come for the wood tomorrow morning at ten o'clock. Dame Hurry-About."

Well! WELL! So all those jobs had been done for nothing—he couldn't wait till tomorrow to have wood for his fire. He would freeze to death in his little cottage. Lazy Luke put the teapot down and began to sniffle.

"Why didn't I get my own wood? Now I've got to go and find some, and I'm so tired and cold. I've walked miles. I've fallen off a bicycle and bumped my head. I've done lots of silly jobs. All because I was too lazy to fetch my own wood! Oooh-hoo-hoo!" And off he went to the woods, crying tears down the front of his suit. Poor Lazy Luke. We could give you some good advice—but what's the use? You'd never take it!

Happy House

JACK, Jane and Benjy lived in a white house with a thatched roof, and a blue front door. It was called Happy House, because it really was a happy house with happy people.

There was Jack, who was nine, and quite a big boy.

There was Jane, who was seven. She had curly hair, and was a great help to Mummy.

There was Benjy, the smallest. He was five. And there was Patter, the sheep-dog puppy, who loved everybody in the house.

There were Mummy and Daddy, and there was Hannah the maid, who kept pots of red and pink and white geraniums on her window-sill.

Next door lived Miss Plum, a round, plump, cosy-looking person, who hadn't liked children at all till she had met Jack,

Jane and Benjy. But she liked them very much. They liked her too, and they liked her cuckoo-clock, her kitten and her musical box as well.

It was summer-time. The sun shone down very hotly, and the sky was as blue as the corn-flowers in Miss Plum's garden. Patter tried to find a cool place to lie down in but he couldn't.

"It's August," said Daddy. "We always go to the seaside in August, but I thought we wouldn't this year, because I have had to spend a lot of money on Happy House. But if you think so, Mummy, we'll go, as it is so very hot."

"Oh *no*!" cried Jane and Benjy. "We can't leave Happy House the very first summer, Daddy!"

"We can paddle every day in the stream if we want to," said Jack. "That's nearly as good as the sea."

"Well, I agree with the children," said Mummy. "I don't want to leave Happy House this year. We'll go to the seaside *next* year."

The children went to tell Miss Plum. They hoped she wasn't going to the seaside either, because they would miss her so.

She was in her garden, in a little tent she had put up. It was striped red and white, and was open in the front to the breeze.

"Oh, you've got a tent!" said Jack. "I'd like a tent too—a wigwam, like the Red Indians have."

"Well, you could come and play Red Indians in *my* tent, when I go out, if you like," said Miss Plum, putting down her knitting. "I know you won't spoil the tent."

"No. Of course we wouldn't," said Jack. "Oh, thanks, Miss Plum. We came to tell you that we're not going away to the seaside this year, and we hope you're not either, because we should miss you."

"Well, I'm not," said Miss Plum. "I've had a letter from

my sister, who lives by the sea. I was going to go and stay with her, but she hasn't been well, so she can't have me."

Miss Plum took up a letter beside her on the garden table. She put on her glasses. "My sister asks me if I will have Tommy and Betty here to stay for a week," she said. "They are my nephew and niece."

"Oh," said Benjy. "Do you like them?"

"Well, you know, I never did like children till you came to live next door to me," said Miss Plum. "I'm afraid I didn't like Tommy or Betty. But perhaps now I know you three children so well, I shall like Tommy and Betty better."

"They can play with us," said Jack, thinking it would be fun to have two more children to play with.

"How old are they?" asked Jane.

"Tommy is eight, and he's a big boy for eight, I remember," said Miss Plum. "And Betty is seven, just your age, Jane."

"Oh well—it will be nice to have them to play with," said Jack.

"I hope you won't leave me out," said Benjy, looking solemn. "You'll all be older than me. I can't help being small."

"We won't leave you out, if you're big and don't cry," said Jack. "You cried again yesterday when you fell down and hurt your knee."

"I saw you had a bandage on," said Miss Plum. "Poor Benjy!"

"Oh, *I* don't mind!" said Benjy, looking brave. "I didn't cry much, anyway."

"You did. You howled," said Jane. Benjy went red and turned away. He was cross.

"Oh, so *that* was the noise I heard!" said Miss Plum. "I thought it must be Patter howling for his dinner, and I was surprised to hear what a wonderful yell he had!"

Everybody laughed, even Benjy. "Patter doesn't howl for his dinner," said Benjy. "He whines. He's so hot to-day, Miss Plum, that he pants all the time as if he's been running."

"And his mouth is too hot to keep his tongue in," said Jane. "So he hangs it out all the time. We all thought it looked very rude at first but now we've got used to it."

"When are Tommy and Betty coming?" asked Jack. "Won't they love the kitten—and your cuckoo-clock—and your musical box!"

"I hope so," said Miss Plum, and she looked rather doubtful. "I'll let you know when they arrive. I *do* hope they behave themselves."

Meeting the Bus

Miss Plum called over the wall to the children three days later. "Jack! Jane! Benjy! I suppose you wouldn't like to go to the bus-stop and meet Tommy and Betty to-day, would you?"

"Oh *yes*," said the three children. "What time are they coming?" asked Jane.

"By the eleven o'clock bus," said Miss Plum. "I've their beds to make, and I would be so glad if you would go and meet them."

Mummy said they could. So, at a quarter to eleven they set off with Patter to the bus-stop. They sat down on the seat and waited. Soon the bus came round the corner and stopped.

Before anyone could get off the bus a boy pushed through the people and jumped down. He was about as big as Jack, but fatter. Then the other people got down, and last of all a little girl with a heavy bag.

"Oh, come on, Betty! You're always last!" said the boy.

"That must be Tommy—and Betty," said Jane. She and Jack and Benjy went to meet them.

"We've come to meet you," said Jane. "Miss Plum, your aunt, asked us to. We live next door."

"And we hope you'll be able to play with us," said Jack.

"Oh, are you Jack, Jane and Benjy?" said the little girl, pleased. "Auntie Sally told us about you."

"Come on, let's go," said Tommy. "You show us the way, Jack."

"Aren't you going to carry your sister's bag?" said Jane, surprised to see Betty dragging the bag by herself.

"Of course not! Betty likes doing things like that for me," said Tommy. "Don't you, Betty?"

"Yes," said Betty. But Jack didn't like to see Betty carrying the bag and he took it from her.

"My daddy says that boys should look after girls, and carry things for them, and help them," said Benjy.

"Pooh! Girls are silly. Let them wait on *us*, that's what *I* say!" said Tommy, and he walked along with his head in the air, looking as if he owned the whole street.

Jack said nothing, but he carried the bag all the way.

"Did you come by yourselves this morning?" asked Jane. "Was it a very long journey?"

"Only about an hour," said Tommy. "That's nothing. I go everywhere by myself. I go out on my bicycle too, and ride for miles."

"Oh—have you got a bicycle?" asked Benjy. "Can you really ride it? Jack can't ride and he's nine."

"I can drive a car too," said Tommy. The others stared at him in astonishment.

"But no one's allowed to till they're sixteen at least," said Jane. "It might even be eighteen. And you're only eight."

"Well, I know how to," boasted Tommy. "I've watched my father heaps of times, and one day when he leaves me in it alone I'm going to start it up and drive it down the street! I can ride a horse too."

"Gracious!" said Benjy, thinking what a wonderful boy Tommy was. "Jack and Jane want to ride, but we can't afford it yet."

"Once I stopped a runaway horse," went on Tommy. "I leapt at his head, hung on to the reins, and dragged him to a standstill. The people all cheered me, I can tell you!"

The others gaped at him. What a remarkable boy! Jack

wished he could say he could do a few things too, but he couldn't think of anything.

"You take a turn at carrying this bag," he said, suddenly. "It's heavy."

"Betty will take it if it's too heavy for you," said Tommy. That made Jack go red. He wouldn't let Betty take it, of course. Daddy would never let Mummy carry anything heavy if he could help it.

"How's old Plummy?" said Tommy. It sounded rude to hear Miss Plum spoken of like that, but it also sounded funny. The children giggled and Tommy was pleased.

"She's a funny old thing, isn't she?" went on Tommy. "Full of 'don'ts' and 'mustn'ts'. Very boring to stay with."

The Happy House children were fond of Miss Plum, and

loyal to her. "She never says don't or mustn't to *us*," said Jane.

"She's not a bit boring," said Jack. "I wish she was *my* aunt."

"She's very, very nice," said Benjy. "I like Plummy."

"Oh, Benjy—don't call her that!" said Jane quite shocked. "Suppose she heard?"

"Well, I think Plummy is a nice name for her," said Benjy. "She *is* like a plum, a nice ripe, juicy, sweet plum. We once thought she ought to be called Miss Plump, because she *is* plump, but I think Plummy's a much better name."

"Here we are," said Jack, opening Miss Plum's gate for Tommy and Betty. "Take the bag now, Tommy. See you later."

"Thanks," said Tommy, and took the bag. "Here, Betty, take it whilst I knock at the door."

"BLIM-BLAM-BLAM!" You should have heard the way Tommy banged on the knocker.

"How *dare* he knock like that!" said Benjy. "Plummy won't like it at all!"

A Game of Red Indians

It rained for the rest of that day and the children did not see any more of Tommy or Betty. But the next day was fine, and they went into the garden.

Tommy was sitting on the top of the wall. "Hallo!" he said. "Come on over and play. We'll play Red Indians and have Plummy's tent for a wigwam."

"Oh, I thought of that too, the other day," said Jack. "Is Miss Plum in?"

"No, she's out," said Tommy. "So it's a good chance to make a noise. She's always saying 'Don't shout!' or 'Shut the door quietly' or something like that. Come along, all of you."

So over the wall they went. Jack and Jane each had Red Indian feather hats, and Benjy had a little band with ordinary feathers stuck into it.

"I'll have your hat," said Tommy to Jane and took it off her head. "Here, you give yours to Betty, Benjy."

"I don't want to," said Benjy. "I don't want to be the only boy without a feather hat."

"Look here, I'm Red-Eagle, the mighty chief," said Tommy, in such an awful voice that Benjy felt quite afraid. "You and Jane are our enemies. I've got to capture you and tie you up. Then I'll run off with Jane. This is my wigwam here."

He pulled Jack and Betty into the tent.

"You're my squaw," he said to Betty. "You keep here and cook my dinner. Jack, you go out and stalk the enemy. Lie flat on your tummy."

He put his head out of the tent. "Benjy and Jane, run away and hide somewhere. Go on!"

It really wasn't a very nice game of Red Indians, because Tommy had all the fun. He ordered Jack and Betty about, he pounced on Jane and Benjy with dreadful yells, and he dragged them to a tree near the tent.

"Tie that brave up!" he ordered Jack, and pointed to Benjy, who didn't look like a brave at all, because he was quite afraid.

Jack tied him up. "Now take that squaw to my tent and guard her," commanded Tommy. "She's mine. I'm going to shoot Benjy and then scalp him."

He danced round the tree, yelling so fiercely that Benjy was scared. Then, to the little boy's horror Red-Eagle took up a bow he had made from a stick and a piece of string. He fitted a wooden arrow into it and took aim at Benjy.

"No, no! You're not to shoot at me!" yelled Benjy. "Jack, Jane! He's shooting at me! Save me!"

Jane rushed out of the tent. "You're not to frighten him!" she said fiercely, to Tommy.

"How *dare* you talk to me like that?" shouted Red-Eagle. "You're only a squaw and you've been captured. Play the game properly or I'll tie you up and shoot you too!"

"Woof!" suddenly said a voice and Patter, the puppy, galloped into the garden. He had been out with Hannah, the maid, but now he was back, longing to join in a game.

"Patter, save me, save me!" shouted Benjy, trying to wriggle free. Red-Eagle gave a wild yell that startled Patter almost out of his skin. He ran to Tommy and growled.

"Call your dog off!" cried Tommy. "I'll shoot him if you don't!"

Then everything became muddled. Benjy broke the string that tied him and rushed to get the bow from Tommy. Jane flew to Patter. Jack fell over Jane and Betty began to howl.

In the middle of it all Tommy let loose the arrow from his bow and it hit Patter on the back. He yelped.

Then all the Happy House children turned on him at once. "You hit Patter! You're cruel!"

"Give me that bow!"

"Oh, Patter, are you hurt?"

Then Mummy's voice came in great astonishment over the wall. "Children! What *is* the matter? Why are you making this dreadful noise?"

Nobody said anything. Jack, Jane and Benjy didn't want to tell tales. Patter barked loudly.

"I'm sorry we've been so noisy," said Tommy, at last. "It's the little ones—and the dog. He made himself a bit of a nuisance. Benjy and Betty are too little to play a game like this. We'll play something quieter."

Mummy went in. Tommy turned with scorn on the others. "Spoiling everything!" he said. "Making such a fuss. And those babies Betty and Benjy howling like that! Silly little cowards!"

Just at that moment Miss Plum came into the garden. She had been out, and had only just come in. She hadn't heard any of the noise at all. She smiled at them all.

"What good children!" she said. "Come along in and drink the ginger-beer I've got for you. Have you had a nice game, Tommy?"

"Lovely," said Tommy. "We're getting on fine, Auntie. The others made me their Red Indian chief, and we had some grand fun. Oh, look—there's the kitten. Couldn't we pretend she's a fox or something and hunt her?"

"No," said Jane, Jack and Benjy all together, glaring at Tommy over their ginger-beer. And for once Tommy said no more!

Tommy Tells A Bad Story

The children didn't like Tommy. They didn't like Betty very much either. They thought she was deceitful.

"She broke one of the wheels off my tiny motor-car," said Benjy. "And she said she didn't."

"And she told Miss Plum that she saw me taking some of the raspberries out of the garden, and I never, never did," said Jane.

"Well, Miss Plum didn't believe her," said Jack. "She knows you wouldn't do a thing like that."

Tommy had plenty of ideas for games but he always wanted his own way and he always wanted to be the chief in everything. His voice was loud, he was strong, and he liked ordering people about.

"He's done so many things, and he's so bold and brave," said Jane. "I wish *you* had done a few things he hasn't done, Jack. He seems to think we're such babies."

"Perhaps we are," said Jack, gloomily. "I've never been in a train alone yet, and he has, heaps of times."

That afternoon the Happy House children didn't play with Tommy and Betty. Mummy said it was time they played quietly by themselves in their own garden for a change. She wanted a rest.

They could hear Tommy and Betty playing next door. It was a game called Burglars and Policemen. Tommy, of course, was the policeman, and Betty was the burglar.

It wasn't a very quiet game. Jack wondered if he had better climb up on the wall and ask Tommy not to yell so much, because his mother was having a rest. But he felt that probably that would only make Tommy shout even more loudly.

Just then there came a crash of glass. It was a very loud noise indeed. It came from Miss Plum's garden. Jack, Jane and Benjy stood still and listened.

They heard nothing after the crash, nothing at all. Not a whisper, not a footstep. What *could* have happened?

Jack sprang up onto the wall. He looked over and saw that the frame in which Miss Plum grew her cucumbers was broken. Three of the panes of glass were smashed in.

No one was in the garden at all. How queer, because Tommy and Betty had been there a few moments before! "I'll jump over and see what's happened to break the glass," said Jack, and he jumped down and went to the frame. A large stone lay in the frame.

Then he heard Miss Plum's voice. "Oh, Jack dear, what has happened? Surely you haven't broken my cucumber frame?"

A voice came out of one of the upstairs windows in Miss Plum's house. It was Tommy's.

"He threw a stone over the wall, Auntie. I saw him from here. Betty and I were reading quietly up here and the noise did make us jump."

"Oh, Jack!" said Miss Plum, looking vexed. "I suppose it was an accident—but how careless of you!"

"I didn't do it, Miss Plum," said Jack. "I just jumped over to see what had happened."

"He's a bad storyteller!" came Betty's voice. "I saw him break the glass!"

Miss Plum said no more. She just went indoors, looking sad and vexed. Jack felt very upset. He looked up at the window but Tommy and Betty were not there any longer. He climbed back over the wall.

Jane was almost in tears, and Benjy looked alarmed. He couldn't believe that anyone could tell such a story. Jane put her arm round Jack.

"You didn't do it," she said. "How *can* Tommy be so bad? *He* must have done it! We didn't see him, it's true, but he and Betty were there just before the crash. They must have tip-toed off to the house at once."

The three children really didn't know what to do. If they went to tell their mother she would hardly believe that Tommy and Betty could tell such stories. And yet it was horrid to think that Miss Plum thought Jack had broken her frame.

"The only thing to do is to go and see Tommy and Betty after tea, and ask them to own up," said Jack. "We've always been taught to own up. Surely they will too, when we tell them what we think of them."

Miss Plum went out after tea. Jane saw her go and went to tell Jack. "We could go and see Tommy and Betty now," she said. "All of us."

So they went in. The side-door was open. Just as they got inside the rain began to fall.

"There's going to be a storm or something," said Jane, looking up at the black sky. "How lovely! I do love storms. I hope there's some lightning."

Tommy and Betty were upstairs in Tommy's room. They didn't seem very pleased to see the three children.

"Look here," said Jack, "you've got to tell your aunt it wasn't me. You know I didn't break that frame. It was you."

"Who told you to come here?" asked Tommy, in a fierce voice. "I'll tell Miss Plum you came in without being asked. I'll tell her you took some of her sweets!"

"You're a bad, wicked boy," said Benjy, suddenly quite shocked.

Tommy turned on Benjy, caught hold of him and shook him hard. "Don't you say things like that to me!" he said. "Do you know what I shall do, if you do? I shall get that Monkey of yours and drown him in the stream. See?"

Monkey was the toy that Benjy loved the best. He yelled when he thought of him drowning in the stream. Tommy was pleased. "And I shall take Angela, Jane's best doll, and break her in two!" he said.

The three children stared at him in despair. How could you make a boy like that own up and do what he ought to do? He wasn't afraid of anything or anyone. He just did what he liked.

The rain struck hard against the window. Then a brilliant flash of lightning came, and lighted up the room, which had gone quite dark.

After that there came a crash of thunder. Jack, Jane and Benjy forgot about the quarrel and ran to the window. They loved a grand storm. Mummy had often let them get out of bed at night and watch one with her.

"What marvellous lightning!" said Jack. "Now—listen for the thunder!"

"Crrrrrrrrash! Rrrrrrumble-rrrroll!" went the thunder, like guns not very far off.

Benjy turned round to tell Betty to come and see. But there seemed to be no one in the room. Where had Betty and Tommy gone?

Then he saw something funny sticking out from under the bed and he stared at it. It was somebody's foot!

"Look, Jane, look, Jack!" cried Benjy. "Tommy's gone under the bed! Oh, he's afraid of the storm! Oh, what a baby he is to be afraid of the thunder and lightning. *I'm* not, and I'm only five!"

The Thunderstorm

JACK and Jane stared in surprise. Yes, it was quite true, Tommy was hiding under the bed, and so was Betty. Well, well, well!

The thunder crashed again. A squeal came from Betty and a moan from Tommy. "Come out, sillies!" cried Jane. "Come out and see the lightning. It's lovely. Don't be such babies!"

Jack, giggling, pulled out Tommy and Betty. What! Was this brave Red-Eagle, the Red Indian chief? Was this the head of all the policemen? Was this the boy who ordered everyone about, and boasted of all he could do?

"Don't go, don't go," begged Tommy, clinging to Jack. "Stay here till the storm is over. Don't leave us."

"Well, we came here to ask you to be decent and own up," said Jack. "And you won't, so it's no good our staying. We'll go."

Tommy burst into tears. He clung to Jack and Jane as if he would never let them go. The lightning flashed again and he moaned.

"You can't leave me, you can't. I'm scared of storms. So's poor Betty. Don't go!"

Betty was sobbing too. She cuddled up to Benjy. "You stay here," she begged. "We're frightened."

"I thought you weren't afraid of anything, Tommy," said Jack.

"Yes, he is. He's afraid of storms and cows and snakes!" wept Betty. "And he's afraid of earwigs too."

"Earwigs!" said Jack. "Fancy being afraid of little insects like that! What a baby he is!"

"He's crying much worse than I ever cry," said Benjy. "Look at him. I hope the lightning and thunder come worse than ever. Jack, don't you think this storm is a punishment for Tommy because he told such a dreadful story about you?"

"I shouldn't be surprised," said Jack, trying to shake himself free from Tommy's hands. "Anyway, we'll go and leave him to his punishment. Mummy will be wondering where we are."

"No, no—*don't* leave me!" wept Tommy. "I'll tell Auntie the truth. I'll tell her it was me and not you. I will, I will."

"Well, I can hear her coming in now," said Jane. "I'll call her."

She went to the top of the stairs and called. "Miss Plum! Is that you? We're up here."

"Oh, are you? Poor children, I hope you are not frightened!" called back Miss Plum. "I'm just coming." She came in and was surprised to see Betty and Tommy in tears.

"They're afraid," said Benjy. "Why are they afraid, Miss Plum? We're not afraid."

"Auntie, don't go out and leave us again!" sobbed Betty. "Another storm might come."

"Tommy's got something to tell you, Miss Plum," said Jack. "Go on, Tommy. Quick!"

Another roll of thunder came and Tommy trembled. He really was a baby! "Oh, Auntie, it wasn't Jack that broke your frame—it was me," he stammered, his cheeks still wet with tears.

His aunt looked at him, and it was not a nice look. "How disgusting of you to put the blame onto someone else," she said. "I'm sorry I asked the children next door to play with you now. I won't ask them again, though perhaps they might be good for you—but instead I'm now afraid you'll be bad for them, and I wouldn't have them spoilt for anything."

Tommy sobbed loudly. He was so ashamed of himself that he hardly knew where to look.

"You had better go straight to bed, both of you," said Miss Plum, in a stern voice that the children had never heard before. "I may perhaps send you home to-morrow. I'm not quite sure. I don't feel as if I want you to stay with me any longer."

Jack, Jane and Benjy thought they had better go. "Goodbye, Miss Plum," they said, in rather small voices.

"Goodbye, dears," said Miss Plum, and went downstairs with them. "I shan't send Tommy and Betty home to-morrow," she said in a low voice. "But I shall send them in to you to say they're sorry, and you can decide whether or not you want to play together any more."

Much Nicer Children

The next morning two miserable-looking children came round the garden-way to Happy House to find Jack and Jane and Benjy. Tommy hung his head, and could hardly look the others in the face.

"We've come to tell you we're sorry," he said. "Oh, Jack how can you like thunderstorms like that? And even little Benjy! I think you're the bravest children I ever knew!"

"No, we're not," said Jack. "Mummy says it all depends on how you're brought up. We asked her. She says if you see grown-ups being scared of anything, you get scared too. But

if you see they don't mind a bit, well, you don't mind either. It's not being brave."

"But I do think you and Betty were babies," put in Benjy.

"Yes. You always boast so much of all the things you can do!" said Jane. "You make yourselves out to be so fine and grand and clever and brave—but all the time you are too frightened even of owning up to something you've done."

"That's much, much worse than being afraid of a thunderstorm," said Jack. "We wouldn't mind a bit being friends with children who were afraid of things—but we don't want to be friends with people who don't tell the truth or are too cowardly to own up to anything."

Tears began to run down Betty's face. "I like you so much," she sobbed. "You're so nice and friendly and kind. I wish we didn't have to go. I wish we had the chance of staying to show you we could be nice too."

"So do I," said Tommy, suddenly, and he turned very red. "I liked you all too. I was just boasting and showing off. I—I can't ride a bicycle—or a horse either. I'm not half as decent as you, Jack, nor half as brave as Benjy here."

The three Happy House children listened in surprise. They suddenly liked Tommy much better than they had ever liked him before.

"Well," said Jack, "you *must* be really brave to say all those things! I should hate to. I wish you were staying now, because we'd play with you again, and be real friends."

"Let's come and ask Miss Plum if they can stay!" said Jane. "No—*I'll* go and ask her! You wait here!" She sped away to find Miss Plum. She was in her sitting-room, doing her flowers.

"Miss Plum! Do let Tommy and Betty stay a bit longer!" cried Jane. "They're sorry for everything now. Really they are. We might teach them a lot of things now, if you'll let

them stay. They'll learn now, but they wouldn't before. Can they stay?"

"Oh, Jane, I hoped you'd come and ask me that!" said Miss Plum, and she kissed her. "You taught them a great lesson yesterday—you and the thunderstorm between you. Maybe you'll make them into nicer children. Yes, they can stay a little longer!"

So Tommy and Betty stayed. And this time it was Jack who was the chief and the leader and the head. It was Jack who ordered everything, and chose everything. He was always just and fair, the best leader there could possibly be.

And Tommy and Betty began to copy him and the others in all they did. They ran errands for Miss Plum without grumbling, and they didn't chase or tease the kitten any more.

When Betty found that Jane had to make her own bed and

the boys' too, she made hers and Tommy's. And she and Tommy found out how much the new glass would be to mend the cucumber frame, and took it from their purses to give Miss Plum.

"Now that really *is* nice of you, my dears!" said Miss Plum. "That really does show me you are sorry and want to do better."

"Well—it was Jane who said we ought to," said Tommy. "We didn't think of it ourselves."

Miss Plum let them take the money to pay the bill for the glass. When they came back there were five enormous ice-creams on the table.

"Go and call the others," said Miss Plum, "it's so hot I thought you would all like a treat!"

Soon Jack, Jane and Benjy were sitting in the cool sitting-

room with Tommy and Betty, enjoying the lovely ice-creams. The kitten came too, but it didn't like the taste of them. Patter loved them, and everyone gave him a bit.

"I ought to have got him one too," said Miss Plum. "I forgot how much he likes them."

Tommy and Betty stayed for four days more. Then they went. "I expect you're glad to see us go!" said Tommy, as Jack, Jane and Benjy went with them to the bus.

"Oh, no! We'll look forward to your coming again!" said Jane. She noticed that this time Tommy was carrying the heavy bag, and not giving it to someone else to take. He had seen how good Jack always was to Jane, his sister, and he was copying him in that too, and trying to be good to Betty.

"Here's the bus!" said Jack. "Well, goodbye. It's been fun playing with you."

"Only the last four days," said Benjy, honestly. "I didn't like it before that. Goodbye!"

"Goodbye—and thanks for everything!" cried Tommy, from the bus.

Jack, Jane, Benjy and Patter went home. They felt quite lonely now that Tommy and Betty had gone. But Hannah was waiting for them with a nice job.

"Here you are at last!" she cried. "Which of you will pick me twelve pounds of ripe greengages from the tree at the bottom of the garden before the wasps get them all? I'm going to make jam to-day!"

Well—what a lovely job! Down the garden they rushed with baskets, and even Patter took one in his mouth!

A Visit to the Farm

One day Jack hurt his foot on a stone, and it made him limp. "It's bruised," said Mummy. "It will be all right in a day or two. You mustn't walk very much on it to-day."

"But it's the day I fetch the eggs and butter for you from the farm," said Jack.

"*I'll* go and get them," said Benjy. "I know the way now."

"No, dear, you're too little," said Mummy.

"Oh, Mummy—yesterday you said I was too big to cry because I got a thorn in my finger and to-day you say I'm too little to go to the farm," said Benjy. "Which am I, little or big? I really would like to know."

Mummy laughed. "You're mixed," she said. "But I couldn't let you go to the farm alone, Benjy dear. It's too far."

"*I'll* go with him," said Jane. "We can fetch the eggs and the butter together. I'll take my pram with Angela in."

"Oh—could Monkey go too?" asked Benjy.

"All right. You get him," said Jane. "I'll get out my pram. We'll have to go by the lane to the farm, because I can't very well take my pram over the fields."

Soon they set off. Angela was sitting up at one end of the pram, and Monkey at the other. "He does so like to see everything we pass," said Benjy. "Can I have a turn at pushing the pram, Jane—just a little turn?"

"Perhaps coming back you can," said Jane. "Angela, look at the red poppies by the wayside. Look out, Benjy, here comes a bicycle."

"I can see it," said Benjy. "You needn't tell me things like that. I'm not Angela. Do you think we shall see Amanda at the farm, Jane?"

Amanda was the farmer's little girl. Patter had come from the farm. Amanda had given him to them, and they always told Amanda all the things he had done, whenever they saw her.

"I wish Patter had come with us," said Jane. "But Jack wanted him. Anyway, he might have chased the hens, like he did last time."

They came to the farm. It was a nice farm with all kinds of noises. The ducks quacked on the pond. The hens clucked everywhere, for they ran about free. A big pig grunted loudly in a sty.

"A farm is nice and noisy and smelly," said Benjy, sniffing in delight. "I shall be a farmer when I grow up."

"You said you were going to be a bus-conductor," said Jane.

"That was yesterday," said Benjy. "To-day I feel as if I'm going to be a farmer. Oh, Jane, there's Amanda. Hi, Amanda, Amanda!"

Amanda was busy. She was cleaning out the hen-house, and she had on a very old and dirty overall. She looked very happy as she poked her head out to see them.

"I'm having a lovely time," she said. "It's a bit smelly, but it's nice to be inside the hen-house. I've sat down in all the nesting-boxes."

"Now don't you let Jane and Benjy get inside the hen-house!" called Amanda's mother. "They're clean, but you aren't, you little scamp. Have you come for the eggs and butter, Jane?"

"Oh, can't we just sit in *one* of the nesting-boxes?" begged Benjy. "I would so like to know what it feels like to be a hen."

"No, not in that clean suit," said Amanda's mother. "If you want to sit in nesting-boxes you must come dirty and in old clothes! And don't you get in the dog's kennel either, as

you did last time, Benjy. Here are the eggs and butter, Jane. Will they go in that lovely doll's pram?"

"Yes. Under the cover," said Jane. "Angela can look after them."

"No. Monkey will," said Benjy.

"They both will," said Amanda's mother, and she tucked the eggs and butter cosily under the pram-cover. "I hope they won't be too heavy for Angela's toes!"

"Amanda, come and look at my pram!" called Jane. But Amanda didn't want to. She didn't like dolls or prams or toys. She liked the dogs and the ducks, the pigs and the cows, and she would clean out any shed or house she was allowed to. Mummy said she was a proper little farmer.

Jane and Benjy set off back home. "We might pick some poppies in the lane," said Benjy. "I like their red petals and their black middles. They have soot in the middle, Jane. I got some on my nose the other day."

"Listen—what's that?" said Jane, stopping. Round the corner of the lane came the sound of boys laughing, and then of something mewing.

Jane was rather afraid of big boys. She wondered whether she would go home another way. But then she heard that mewing sound again, and she thought she would go and see what it was.

So she hurried round the corner with Benjy and the pram. She saw three boys there, bigger than Jack. In the corner by the hedge they had a little black kitten.

One of the boys was trying to hold the kitten down, and another boy was tying something to its tail. It was a tin-lid on a long bit of string.

"Now, when we let the kitten go, it will run off and drag the lid behind it!" said one of the boys. "My word, it will get such a fright that it will go like lightning!"

"Mew-ew-ew——!" said the kitten, in a piteous little voice.

The Little Black Kitten

Jane forgot all about being afraid of big boys. She pushed the pram-handle into Benjy's hands and rushed up to the three boys.

"What are you doing? Leave that little kitten alone! You bad, wicked boys!"

The boys looked at her and laughed. One of them pushed her away. "It's not *your* kitten!" said the boy. "It's a stray! Doesn't belong to anyone."

"It's *my* kitten!" suddenly said Jane, in a very loud voice. Benjy was filled with surprise. Whatever did Jane mean? It wasn't her kitten! They hadn't got a kitten. Jane was telling a story!

" 'Tisn't," said a boy.

"I tell you it *is*!" said Jane and she stamped her foot. "And I'm going straight to the policeman to tell him you're hurting my kitten! Let it go!"

The boys had finished tying the lid to the little thing's tail now. They let it go. It shot away, and the tin-lid jumped after it with a clatter. The kitten was terrified.

"Mew-ew-ew!" she said, and rushed on in fear. The tin-lid raced behind her, tied to her tail. The kitten was so frightened that she didn't look where she was going—and she ran straight into a little pond by the wayside. Splash! In she went. The boys laughed. Jane cried out and rushed to the little pond. She had to wade in and get the kitten, which was almost drowning.

"Now, what's going on here?" suddenly said a grown-up's voice. "Bill—Harry—Walter—are you teasing that little girl?"

"They were hurting the kitten!" yelled Benjy. "They're wicked and cruel. Jane's got the kitten out of the pond. Jane, Jane, wait, I'm coming."

He hurried to Jane with the pram. The three boys were getting a fine scolding from the man, but Benjy didn't bother to stop and hear it. He wanted to get to Jane.

Jane was crying. "Oh, the poor little thing," she said. "Look, Benjy, it's trembling and shivering, and it's as wet as can be. Oh, we must take it home and dry it."

"Put it into the pram," said Benjy. "I'll take Monkey and Angela out and carry them. Put it into the pram and cover it up. Oh, Jane, you *are* brave!"

"I'm not," wept Jane. "Just see how I'm crying. But I can't stop, because I'm so sorry for the kitten. How can people do those things?"

Benjy took Monkey and Angela out of the pram. He moved the butter and eggs to the end. Then Jane put the trembling kitten into the pram and covered it up. It lay quite still and good.

"Mummy will know what to do," said Benjy, trying to comfort Jane. "She always knows. Don't cry, Jane."

They wheeled the kitten home. Jane wiped her eyes and stopped crying. Benjy trotted beside her with Monkey and Angela. It was very exciting to have a kitten in the pram, he thought.

As soon as Jane got to the gate she called Mummy and Jack. "Come here quickly," she said. "Do come!"

So they came—and when Jane pulled back the cover of the pram and showed them the wet, trembling kitten, they could hardly believe their eyes.

Benjy and Jane told them all about it. Mummy gently lifted the kitten out and sat down with it in her lap. "Go and get a warm towel from the linen cupboard," she said to Jane. "And you, Benjy, ask Hannah for a little warm milk. We will soon have the kitten right."

She untied the string from its tail. When Jane brought the warm towel she gently rubbed the kitten dry. It let her do what she wanted. It knew she wouldn't hurt it or tease it.

"There!" said Mummy, and set it gently down on the ground. "It's dry. What a funny, thin little thing it is. Is that the milk, Hannah? Thank you. Now, kitten, lap it up."

The kitten went to the milk and lapped every drop with its tiny pink tongue. The children watched it. After it had lapped it sat down and began to wash its face.

"Oh, hasn't it got good manners!" said Jane. "Washing after meals like that. Look, Benjy, it uses its paw like a sponge, wiping its face round and round."

"I wish we could keep it," said Jack. "I do so love kittens. It hasn't got a home, Mummy. I do wish we could keep it."

"Mummy—I told a dreadful story to those boys," said Jane, suddenly. "Oh, Mummy, I don't know why I did, because you know I don't tell untruths."

"Yes, I heard you tell that story," said Benjy, remembering. "You gave me a surprise, Jane."

"I gave myself a surprise," said Jane, and she looked at Mummy with rather a red face. "Mummy, I wanted to stop those boys from teasing the kitten, and I told them it was *my* kitten. I knew it wasn't, but I said it was."

Mummy looked at Jane's anxious red face, and she smiled. She picked up the kitten and put it into Jane's arms. "Funny little girl!" she said. "It *is* your kitten! You shall have it and keep it. You thought it was a story, but it wasn't—because it is your very own kitten! You made it yours!"

"Oh, *Mummy*!" said Jane, and buried her face in the kitten's soft fur. "Thank you! It didn't belong to anyone, it was just a stray. And now it's mine. You're mine, kitten, my very own."

"Can I have a share of it?" asked Benjy.

"Yes, you can—and Jack, too. It shall be the Happy House kitten, like Patter is the Happy House dog," said Jane, joyfully. "Oh, listen—it's purring! It *likes* belonging to us!"

Patter and Jumpy

"WHERE's Patter?" said Jack. "He was here with me before you came in. We'll show him the kitten."

But Patter had gone after the butcher-boy down the road. He loved the butcher-boy. He thought he smelt nicer than anyone in the world.

"The only thing that worries me is if Patter will hurt the kitten," said Jane, looking anxious. "It would be dreadful if Patter teased it. Poor little thing, it has had enough teasing."

"Patter chases hens sometimes," said Benjy. "He might chase the kitten."

"We'll have to tie him up," said Jack.

"Oh, he'll be unhappy," said Benjy. "We'll have to keep the kitten indoors, in our playroom. We can shut the door. Then Patter won't be able to tease it."

"It's going to have a black, black coat," said Jane, and she stroked it. "Soft as silk. And it's got green eyes. Hark at it purring. I wish I could purr."

"I wish I could too," said Benjy, and he tried.

"Don't do that. You're frightening the kitten," said Jane. "What shall we call it?"

"Blackie," said Benjy. "Nigger. Sooty. Green-Eyes. Paddy-Paws."

"Don't think of so many names at once," said Jane. "You muddle me. *I'm* going to choose its name. It's *my* kitten. But I just can't think of one at the moment."

"Oh, here's Patter," said Jack. "I'll catch him and hold him. I won't let him get near the kitten."

He caught Patter and held him. Patter scented the kitten

and tried to get to it to smell it. But Jack wouldn't let him.

"You're not to frighten the kitten," he told Patter. "If you do we'll be cross with you."

They took the kitten into the playroom and shut the door. Patter whined outside. Benjy couldn't help feeling rather sad for him.

The kitten became very lively. It leapt about and chased its own tail. It jumped onto the top of the bookcase and down again. It jumped up to a chair, chased its tail there and fell off. Then it jumped onto Jane's knee and played with a button on her frock.

"You're very jumpy!" said Jane, tickling it. "A jumpy little kitten. Oh—Jack, that's what I'll call it—Jumpy!"

"That's a very *good* name for a kitten," said Jack and Benjy nodded. "Yes, lovely. Jumpy, Jumpy, Jumpy! Do you like your name?"

The kitten lay on Jane's knee and purred. "Jumpy, you're our own kitten now," said Jane. "We've got Patter and Jumpy. What nice names they sound together—Patter and Jumpy. Patter patters about, and Jumpy jumps about!"

Patter whined outside. "I'll go and play with him," said Benjy. "I don't want him to feel left out. I know what a horrid feeling that is."

So he slipped out to play with Patter down by the stream at the end of the garden, whilst Jane and Jack played with the black kitten.

Everyone was pleased about the kitten. Mummy loved it. Daddy was amused with it too. As for Hannah, she was delighted.

"I'm sure there's a mouse in the larder," she said, "and I'll be glad to have a kitten growing up to catch it."

The children were very careful to keep Patter away from the kitten. They were so afraid he might bite it or chase it.

"If he frightens Jumpy, she might run away and never come back," said Benjy.

One day, after they had had their dinner, the children went into the playroom to find Jumpy. She wasn't there. Jane pointed to the window.

"We left the window open," she said. "Jumpy must have gone out—and, oh dear, Patter was in the garden. I do hope he hasn't bitten her!"

Mummy came in and heard. She looked out into the garden and then she laid her hand on Jane's arm. "Don't open the garden door yet," she said. "Look out there!"

The children looked out into the garden. They saw Patter

lying down asleep. They saw Jumpy creeping quietly up to him, not in the least afraid!

And then Jumpy leapt right up to Patter and banged him hard on his nose with her paw! Before Patter knew what it was that had wakened him Jumpy was half-way up a tree. Patter growled and put his head down again. He shut his eyes.

Down the tree came Jumpy, very quietly. She crept up to Patter and jumped at his tail. He awoke again and leapt up. He raced round to Jumpy.

But did Jumpy run away? Not a bit of it! She sat up on her hind-legs and smacked the puppy on the nose again!

"Woof!" barked Patter in surprise. He made as if he was going to dart at Jumpy. The kitten ran away and Patter chased her. Up a tree she went, and Patter couldn't reach her.

As soon as Patter had sat down again the kitten dropped on to his back. Mummy began to laugh.

"I don't think we need worry about Patter teasing Jumpy," she said. "I think it will be the other way round. Jumpy will tease poor Patter!"

"She's not a bit afraid of him," said Jane, laughing too, as she saw Jumpy trying to play with Patter's tail. "And she'll always be able to jump out of his way if he gets cross. Oh, Mummy—aren't they funny together! Can we let them always be together now, if they want to?"

"Oh yes," said Mummy, and she opened the door that led into the garden. "We needn't be afraid that Patter will worry Jumpy—we shall just have to be careful that Jumpy doesn't scare Patter!"

Patter and Jumpy both came racing across the grass as soon as they heard the playroom door open. Patter licked everyone's legs. Jumpy pounced on Mummy's shoes. They were a mad little couple!

Jumpy grew plump and her coat shone like black silk. Her

eyes were still as green as Miss Plum's cucumbers, and she had long white whiskers. She was the lovingest, liveliest, naughtiest kitten any family could wish for.

And very soon at night, when Patter lay down in his basket, Jumpy crept in too! She put her little black arms round his big head and slept there, warm and safe with him. How Benjy loved to see them like that!

A Very Hot Day

THE first days of September were so hot that the children wore only little sun-suits and shady hats. Benjy didn't want to wear a hat, because he said it made his hair stick together.

"You'll get sun-stroke if you don't," said Jane. "You'll be sick and go pale and get the most dreadful headache you can imagine, and be in bed for days."

"How do you know?" asked Benjy.

"Because Amanda told me," said Jane. "She got sun-stroke last year when she went out in the fields all day without a hat."

After that Benjy thought he would wear a hat. He worried

about Jumpy and Patter, in case they got sun-stroke too. But Mummy said animals never did.

"You go out with Hannah and help her bring back the shopping," said Mummy. "Take Patter with you. He would like that, especially as you are going to the butcher's."

So Benjy took a basket and went with Hannah and Patter. Hannah said she would go by the toy-shop and let him look in.

Jane finished her jobs, and Jack came back from the farm with the eggs and butter he had been to fetch. His foot was quite better now. Miss Plum looked over the wall.

"I wish I was like you and could wear only a sun-suit," she said. "Why don't you bathe in your stream? It's lovely and clean, you know."

"Oh, what a good idea!" said Jane, and ran to ask Mummy. Mummy said yes, she didn't see why they shouldn't, but they

mustn't put their heads under the water in case it wasn't good to swallow.

Soon Jane and Jack were sitting down in the stream. They splashed one another. It was fun. Jumpy came and watched them but she wouldn't go near the water. She was afraid of water since she had jumped into the pond when the bad boys had teased her.

"I think I'll undress Angela and put a sun-suit on her," said Jane. "She'd like that. Oh—and do you think Monkey would like a bathe, too, Jack?"

"Yes. But you'd better wait till Benjy comes back," said Jack, picking up a pebble with his toes. "Look, Jane, I can pick up stones with my toes."

But Jane had gone indoors to fetch Angela. The doll was in the playroom, sitting up in her cot. Monkey was there too,

sitting on the window-sill, looking out of the window. Benjy always said Monkey liked to look out of the window.

Jane undressed Angela quickly. She had a little knitted suit for her to wear, that looked very like Jane's own sun-suit. "There!" said Jane. "You look sweet—and soon you will feel nice and cool, Angela."

She stopped by Monkey. Surely he would like to bathe too? Well, perhaps not *really* bathe, but just wear a sun-suit and sit and watch her and Jack and Angela?

She found an old red vest belonging to a doll and put it on Monkey. Then she carried him and Angela out to the stream.

Angela had a strong rubber body and was a doll you could bath. So she was quite all right to put into the water. Jane sat her down carefully.

"It feels a tiny bit cold at first," she told her. "But it soon feels lovely. Oh, Angela, you look sweet!"

Jack splashed Angela. "She doesn't mind!" said Jane. "She's brave. Look, I've brought Monkey too. Doesn't he look funny in this old red vest!"

Jack didn't bother about Monkey and he soon got tired of Angela. He lay down in the water.

"Don't let it get into your mouth, Mummy said," said Jane. "Oh, Jack, there's a fish!"

That made Jack sit up. He and Jane sat quite quiet to make the water still again. They were in a kind of little pool with the stream flowing beyond them.

"I can see the fish again," said Jane, in a whisper. "I'll reach back and get a twig of something, Jack, and point him out to you."

She reached behind her without looking—and, oh dear, her arm bumped against Monkey, who was sitting on a nearby stone—and he lost his balance and fell right into the water.

Benjy Loses His Temper

"GOODNESS! There goes Monkey!" cried Jane, and tried to fish him out. He was very very wet.

"Well, he's soaked now, so you might as well let him finish his bathe," said Jack, lazily. Jane sat him down in the water again and laughed.

"He looks sort of surprised," she said. "Won't Benjy laugh when he sees him!"

But Benjy didn't laugh. He came running down to the stream with Patter, ready to tell about the things in the toy-shop—and he suddenly saw Monkey in the water!

Monkey had fallen on his face, and was lying like that in the stream, his long arms waving about in the water.

Benjy gave such a squeal that Jane and Jack jumped.

"Oh! Look at *Monkey*! Who put him there? He's drowning, he's drowning!"

"He's not," said Jane, and she sat Monkey up. He fell

forward again and dabbled his face in the water. Benjy jumped into the stream with a splash, almost on top of Angela.

"You bad girl!" Benjy shouted to Jane. "How dare you take *my* Monkey out and put him a red vest on, and drown him in the water? I'll smack you till you cry!"

And, to Jane's enormous surprise, the little boy fell on her and began to slap her as hard as he could. Slap, slap, slap! Benjy went quite mad, and, as Jane was sitting down in the water, it was difficult for her to stop him.

In the middle of all this, just as Jack was getting up to stop Benjy, Mummy came. When she saw what Benjy was doing, she was very angry.

"Benjy! Stop at once! I will not have this behaviour. Go indoors at once."

Benjy stopped. He faced his mother, red in the face and panting. "She's a bad girl!" he sobbed. "Do you know what she did? She . . ."

"I don't want to hear anything," said Mummy. "What you did is quite enough. Go indoors and go up to bed."

"But it isn't fair!" cried Benjy, and he stamped his foot in the water and splashed everyone. "I want to tell . . ."

"GO INDOORS AT ONCE!" said Mummy, and her voice sounded so stern that Benjy was shocked. He came out of the water. The tears poured down his cheeks.

"I shall never like Jane again!" he shouted. "Never! I shall never like anyone again! I shall go indoors and I shall go to bed, but I shan't ever speak to any of you again!"

He tore up the garden, went into the playroom, slammed the door and went up the stairs, leaving little drips of water as he went. He was very angry and very hurt and very miserable. He suddenly remembered Monkey. Why, he had left him in the stream. Oh, would that horrid horrid Jane take him out?

He looked out of the window. He saw Mummy coming up

the garden. She had Monkey. She was squeezing the water out of him. Poor, poor Monkey. He must hate that. Perhaps Mummy would bring Monkey up to him.

But she didn't. She didn't come near him. She was angry, and she wasn't often angry, Benjy knew.

He suddenly felt tired. He threw off his sun-suit and got into bed. He lay down under a sheet, and sighed heavily. "I shall never be happy again," said Benjy, out loud. "Never. I wish I didn't belong to this family. It's a horrid family. I

don't like any of them. I shall run away and then they'll be very, very sorry."

A tear rolled down his cheek again. "They'll never hear of me again after I've run away. I shan't let them know what happens to me. I'll leave them all, horrid, unkind things!"

Benjy fell asleep. He awoke when Hannah came into the room with some dinner on a tray.

"Your mother says you must stay up here till you feel sorry for slapping Jane, and then you can come down and say so," said Hannah. "Really, Benjy, I'm surprised at you!"

"I don't like you either," said Benjy. "And I shan't eat any dinner. You can take it away. You're a horrid person too."

But Hannah didn't take the dinner away and he did eat it after all. Then, because it was so very hot, he fell asleep again.

Hannah came in with a tray of tea. It was quite a nice tea. "Now why don't you be a good boy and let me brush your hair for you, and take you downstairs to tea?" she said.

"Where's Monkey?" asked Benjy.

"He's hanging on the line to dry," said Hannah. "You can see him if you look."

Benjy was off the bed in a trice. He looked out of the window and, oh dear, there was poor, poor Monkey hanging by his tail to dry!

"What a cruel thing to do to him!" said Benjy, upset. "He's upside down—and pegged by his tail too. He must be feeling dreadful. Go and get him, Hannah."

"Not if you talk like that!" said Hannah, in a huff, and went out. Benjy ate his tea, and sulked, and wanted Monkey.

Suddenly the door opened and Jane peeped in the room. "Oh, Benjy," she said. "Oh, Benjy, they've pegged Monkey on the line. I've just seen him. He's so miserable."

"Jane, Jane! Get him for me!" begged Benjy. "Please, please do! Oh, Jane, I can't bear to see him there either. It wasn't his fault he got wet."

"No. It was mine," said Jane. "But it was an accident. He fell in."

"Oh," said Benjy. "Well, please, Jane, go and get Monkey for me."

Jane went out of the room. She ran down the stairs and into the garden. There was no one there. Benjy watched her unpeg Monkey quickly. He hugged himself for joy.

"Dear Jane!" he said. "Dear kind Jane! Now I shall soon have Monkey!"

Jane came in with Monkey. He still felt rather damp. Jane sat on the bed with Benjy, and they tried to warm Monkey together.

"Thank you, Jane, oh thank you!" said Benjy. "You're the kindest girl!"

Then he remembered how he had slapped Jane, and he

looked at her. "Jane! I'm sorry I slapped you. It was only because I thought you were drowning Monkey."

"As if I *would*!" said Jane. "I love Monkey as much as you do. He used to go to bed with *me* before you had him. I tell you, he fell in. I put him on a stone to watch me and Jack and Angela. He was waiting for you."

"I didn't know that," said Benjy, and he looked sad and ashamed. "I lost my temper and I hit you, and I know I should never hit a girl. Are you very angry, Jane?"

"No, not now," said Jane. "I know how you must have felt when you thought I was drowning Monkey—like *I* felt when I saw those boys teasing poor Jumpy. It's all right, Benjy. I love you again."

"And I love my family again," said Benjy, happily. "I shan't run away after all. I nearly did, Jane."

"You always say that," said Jane. "Come on downstairs and have some plums. We've been picking them."

So Benjy went downstairs with Jane. "I've said I'm sorry," he said to Mummy. "And I am. I won't do it again."

"Well, come and sit by me and I'll find you a ripe plum," said Mummy. "Is Monkey dry yet? Almost. Sit him in the sunshine again, but don't give him any plum or he'll get sticky."

It was nice sitting there in the sun. Mummy was sewing. Jack was making paper-boats. Jane was playing with Jumpy and Patter. Hannah was humming in the kitchen.

"I couldn't possibly run away from this nice family," said Benjy to Mummy. "I've been silly and bad. I'll be extra good now and make up for it. Jane was so nice to go and fetch Monkey for me."

Miss Plum looked over the wall. "What a nice happy

family you all look, sitting together in the evening sun!" she called.

"Yes!" called back Mummy. "Even Benjy thinks he won't run away from us after all! *Isn't* that a good thing?"

And how everybody laughed—Benjy too!

A Picnic on Breezy Hill

"WE'LL go for a picnic, I think," said Daddy one Saturday. "We'll go in the car to Breezy Hill, and feel the wind on our faces. Can you pack us up a nice lunch, Mummy?"

The children were pleased. They all loved a picnic. "You shall come too, Patter," said Jane.

"And Jumpy as well?" asked Benjy. "Jumpy doesn't like to be left out."

"No, not Jumpy," said Mummy. "You can't take cats on a picnic."

"What a pity!" said Benjy. "Jumpy will be lonely. Is Hannah coming too?"

"Yes, we'll take Hannah as well," said Mummy. "She will love it. I'll go and get the picnic hamper ready."

The picnic hamper was almost as big as the laundry basket! It had belonged to Daddy's family, and as they had been a big family and had often gone for picnics, they had had to have an enormous hamper.

Now Daddy has the hamper for his own little family. It took pork-pies and ham, tarts and sandwiches, apples and ginger-beer quite easily.

"We can stuff the corners with paper," said Mummy. She and Hannah cut sandwiches quickly. Patter and Jumpy came to watch them. Patter was excited. He liked the smell of pork-pies and he liked to know they were all going for a picnic. Perhaps he could chase a rabbit!

Jumpy sat on the window-sill and watched everything. She jumped down and tried to jump on to the table but Hannah sent her down. She wasn't allowed on any table at all.

"*Can't* Jumpy come with us?" begged Benjy. "Just this once? She does so want to. She'll feel dreadful left behind, without even Hannah or Patter here."

"She'll curl up in the sun and sleep all the time," said Hannah.

"She won't. Look how wide awake she is!" said Benjy.

"Now you go away and don't come bothering," said Hannah. "And take your fingers out of that meat-paste. Ah, it's no wonder the kitten comes to you and you all over potted meat!"

"Mummy, can we shut Jumpy up in the play-room, with Patter's basket to sleep in, and her ball to play with?" asked Benjy. "Just so she won't feel too bad?"

"Yes, we'll do that," said Mummy. "Now go away before you upset the milk."

At last everything was ready. Daddy had got the car out.

The hamper was put in the back of it. Patter was sitting on the back seat with Jack. Hannah was putting on her hat. Mummy was locking the back door.

"Mummy—I can't find Jumpy," said Benjy, appearing in the kitchen, looking worried.

"Well, she's somewhere about," said Mummy. "I shooed her down from the table again, the last time I saw her."

"Well, I want to put her in the play-room, with Patter's basket and her ball," said Benjy. "I've got them all ready."

"Oh dear, Benjy, don't begin worrying about Jumpy!" said Mummy. "She can look after herself now!"

"She can't," said Benjy. "Just suppose we left her out-of-doors, Mummy—it might rain—or a strange dog might come in and chase her—or someone might come and steal her."

"Well, you've got two minutes to look for her, and then, if you haven't found her, you must leave her and get in the car," said Mummy. "Or else you will be left behind."

Poor Benjy! He couldn't find Jumpy anywhere and he really was very nearly left behind. He heard Daddy starting up the car, and just ran down the path in time.

"I do think you're unkind to leave poor Jumpy like this," he said. "I feel upset about her."

"I do a bit too," Jane said to him. "I hope that big dog down the road doesn't come in and get her."

This was a most alarming thought. Benjy's face grew very long indeed.

"I shan't enjoy the picnic now," he thought. "I shan't want any of those lovely tarts to eat!"

It was lovely up on Breezy Hill. Benjy forgot about Jumpy as he tore up and down. But he remembered again when they all sat down to their lunch, and Daddy put the picnic basket down in the middle of them.

"I've remembered Jumpy," said Benjy, sadly. "I thought I heard a mew just then, and it reminded me."

"I thought I heard a mew too," said Jane. Mummy laughed.

"What dreadful children you are! I expect Jumpy is at this very moment having a lovely game with Miss Plum's kitten next door," said Mummy.

And then *everyone* heard a *mew*! It was most extraordinary. Mummy looked all round but she couldn't see a cat.

"Do you think it's Jumpy in trouble at home and calling for help?" said Jane.

"Don't be silly, Jane," said Mummy, and opened the hamper. She had stuffed the empty corners with paper, as she had said she would. She pulled them out—and my goodness, what was this coming out with the paper?

Yes—it was Jumpy! "Mew-ew-ew!" she said, in a pleased little voice. Benjy gave a yell of joy.

"She came after all! She got into the hamper so that she could come! Isn't she clever? Oh, Jumpy, I *knew* I heard you mew!"

"Mew-ew-ew! Mew-ew-ew!" said Jumpy, rubbing herself against Benjy's knee.

"She says, 'I meant to come with you-oo-oo,' " explained Benjy, and everyone laughed.

"So we've got the whole of Happy House folk after all!" said Mummy, dealing out sandwiches. "Me—and Daddy—and Hannah—and Jack—and Jane—and Benjy—and Patter—and Jumpy too!"

"Now I'm happy, and so is Jane," said Benjy, giving Jumpy some of his meat-paste sandwich. "There's only one thing I like better than leaving Happy House and going for a picnic."

"What's that?" asked Mummy.

"Why, leaving the picnic and going back to dear old Happy House, of course!" said Benjy. "I should have thought you could have guessed *that*, Mummy!"

"Perhaps I did!" said Mummy, and she smiled her nicest smile. "Yes—I really think I did!"

The Coming of the Circus

"HIE, Susy-Ann, Susy-Ann, come here!" yelled a small boy. "There's a circus coming into the next field. Come and watch!"

"Oh, Pip, is there really?" cried an excited voice, and a little girl ran out of a tumble-down old cottage and joined the boy in the garden at the back.

"Yes, look!" said Pip, and he pointed to the golden buttercup field. Susy-Ann saw that gay caravans and big travelling cages and carts were passing through the gate into the field.

"Let's go and sit on the fence and watch," said Pip. So off they went. Behind Susy-Ann trotted a snow-white goat with a long beard. All three went to the fence. The children climbed up and sat on the top and the goat stuck his head through the bars of the fence.

"Mister Binks wants to watch too," said Susy-Ann, and she patted her goat, who drew back his upper lip and pretended to nibble the little girl's leg.

It was very exciting watching the circus getting into the field. There was a lot of shouting and yelling, a great deal of running about, and beckoning. One by one all the caravans got through the gate, and the big travelling cages too.

"Look! Elephants!" said Pip, and he pointed to where three enormous beasts stood under some great elm trees at the farther end of the field. "Oh, Susy-Ann! Aren't they big?"

"Look! There's a boy about as tall as you," said Susy-Ann. "He belongs to the circus. Isn't he lucky?"

They watched the boy. He had ginger hair that shone in the sun, and his face was so covered with freckles that it was difficult to see a place without one! He was whistling cheerily as he went, carrying two buckets, slung across his shoulders on a wooden bar.

"Hallo, kids!" said the circus boy. "Tell me where I can get some water."

"There's a stream in the field over there," said Pip. "But if you like you can use our well. It's just here."

"Oh, thanks very much," said the boy, and he went to the well. He sent the bucket down the well, wound it up again full of water, and tipped it into one of his own big buckets.

"I'll help you," said Pip, and he went to turn the handle. "Do you belong to the circus?"

"Rather!" said the freckled boy.

"What do you do?" asked Susy-Ann shyly.

"What *don't* I do!" said the boy. "I do everything—fetch the water, groom the horses, oil the elephants, feed the chimpanzees, scatter the sawdust on the ring, clear up afterwards. . . . My word, I'm the most important person in the circus, and don't you forget it!"

The two children laughed. The circus boy had the cheekiest twinkle in his green eyes.

"Are you coming to see our circus?" asked the boy, lifting his two full buckets. "It's a jolly good one! You should see the chimpanzees riding their bicycles!"

"Oooh!" said Pip and Susy-Ann.

"And you should see the three elephants playing hockey!" said the boy.

Pip and Susy-Ann wished they could. They stared at the freckled circus boy and wished with all their hearts that they belonged to the circus too.

"I don't suppose we can come," said Pip. "We never have any money."

The boy set down his buckets again. "Listen," he said, "if you . . ."

But a loud shout from the circus field stopped him. "JERRY! JERRY! If you don't bring that water at once I'll come after you with a stick!"

"Goodbye!" said Jerry, with a grin. "I must go. They can't do without me for a minute, as you see! I'll be busy till tonight. Come and see me then. I'll look out for you. So long, kids!"

He went off carrying his buckets. The children watched him take them to a big blue caravan where a plump woman was waiting for them.

"That must be his mother," said Susy-Ann.

"He's lucky to have one!" said Pip. "I wish we had! I say—won't it be fun to go and find Jerry tonight!"

"Can my goat go too, do you think?" asked Susy-Ann, patting Mister Binks. "He won't like being left behind."

"Mister Binks will come whether we say he can or not," said Pip. "That goat follows you everywhere, Susy-Ann. If only he didn't eat everything the way he does!"

"He ate a duster off the clothes-line next door yesterday," said Susy-Ann. "I do hope Mrs. Jones won't scold me for it."

The children longed for the evening to come. All that day they watched the circus camp settling into the field. The caravans were together, smoke rising from their little chimneys. All their doors at the back were wide open. The caravan folk ran up and down their steps, shouted to one another, and enjoyed the May sunshine.

The elephants still stood under the big elm trees in the shade. An enormous tent was being put up in the middle of the field, where the show was going to be given. Near the tent were the animal cages. It was a gay scene, and Pip and Susy-Ann loved watching it all.

At last the evening came. The two children ran down their garden, climbed over the fence at the back, and there they were, in the circus field! It did feel exciting.

"I wonder where Jerry is," said Susy Ann. "Oh, Mister Binks, you shouldn't have come! How did you squeeze through the fence?"

The goat snorted and wagged his beard. He pressed close to the little girl and would not go away.

"There's Jerry!" said Pip. And sure enough there was the ginger-haired boy, jumping down the steps of his blue caravan, waving to them.

"Hallo!" he said. "Isn't it hot? Let's go and sit under the hedge and smell the may. I've got some buns for us to eat."

The three children sat down and munched their buns. Mister Binks snorted, but there was no bun for him. So he ate the paper bag in which Jerry had brought the buns.

"I say, look at that! He's eaten the bag!" said Jerry in surprise. "Will he be ill?"

"*Ill!*" said Pip scornfully. "Good gracious! If Mister Binks ate a coal-scuttle full of coal he wouldn't be ill. He might get hiccups, perhaps—but he certainly wouldn't be ill."

"What a marvellous goat!" said Jerry. "And what a funny name he's got!"

"Susy-Ann called him Mister Binks," said Pip. "She thought he looked just like an old man who lives opposite to us and has a white beard like her goat."

Jerry rolled over and laughed. Mister Binks sniffed at him, but Jerry pushed him away. "No," he said, "you're *not* going to eat my hair. It may look like carrots, but it's not!"

That made Pip and Susy-Ann laugh.

"There's a boy we know with hair like yours, and everybody calls him Carrots!" said Susy-Ann.

"I fight anybody who calls me Carrots or Ginger," said Jerry.

"Oh," said Pip. He looked at Jerry and thought he would be a very good fighter. He made up his mind never to call him Carrots or Ginger. Jerry was a much nicer name.

"What are *your* names?" asked Jerry, sitting up again.

"My name's Philip, but I'm called Pip. And she's called Susy-Ann," said Pip. "She's my little sister. We haven't got a mother. And our father's going away to Australia without us, so we soon shan't have a father either!"

"That's bad luck!" said Jerry, staring at them. "I've got a mother *and* a father, and they're both fine. But I say—what are you going to do when your father's gone away?"

"We're going into a Home for poor children," said Pip. "And the dreadful part is that I'm to be sent to a Boys' Home and Susy-Ann is to go to a Girls' Home. So we shall hardly ever see one another again."

Susy-Ann gave a great sob. Pip put his arm round her. "Cheer up!" he said. "Perhaps you can take Mister Binks with you."

Susy-Ann felt sure she couldn't. It would be so dreadful not to have Pip or Mister Binks. The little girl felt very miserable. Jerry looked at her shining golden head and thought she was like a small sad doll. He felt miserable too, for he was a kind-hearted boy. He wondered what he could do to make the two children happier.

"Don't cry, Susy-Ann," he said. "Listen! I'll get you into the big tent to see the show one night! How would you like that?"

"Oooh yes, Jerry!" said Susy-Ann, her wet eyes shining with joy. Mister Binks pushed Pip away and licked the tears off Susy-Ann's cheeks. They tasted salt, and the goat liked them.

"Don't!" said Susy-Ann, and she tried to push the goat away. "Oh, Jerry, I would so love to see the circus! And so would Pip."

"Well, I'll manage one night before we leave here," said Jerry. "We are here for ten days. How long is it before you have to go away to your new homes?"

"We go in ten days too," said Pip. "We haven't very long now. Please don't cry again, Susy-Ann. Look—you can hold my white mouse for a bit if you like."

The boy made a peculiar squeaking noise, exactly like the squeal of a mouse. Jerry stared at him in astonishment. A small white mouse with pink eyes poked its head out of Pip's left sleeve.

"I say! Look at that! Does that mouse live up your sleeve all day long?" said Jerry.

"Yes," said Pip. "Or somewhere about me. She's called Snowball. You can hold her, Susy-Ann."

The little girl loved holding the tiny, cuddlesome mouse. She made a little home for her in her two hands, and Snowball snuggled there, her nose woffling up and down and her white whiskers twitching.

"Can I hold her after Susy-Ann?" asked Jerry. "I say, isn't she sweet! I wish I had a mouse like that!"

But before Jerry could have his turn at holding Snowball he had to go. His father called him and he jumped up.

"Come again to-morrow and bring Snowball and Mister Binks!" he called.

Pip and Susy-Ann see the Circus

EVERY day the three children met and talked and played. The circus show had opened and was doing well. Crowds of people went to see it every night, and Jerry told Pip and Susy-Ann that Mr. Phillipino, who owned the circus, was very pleased.

"Sometimes we don't do at all well," said Jerry. "If it's a rainy week and nobody wants to turn out at night to come to a wet field we don't get much money. Then we have to go short of food if we haven't saved any money for a bad time!"

Mister Binks the goat snorted, and Pip laughed.

"Mister Binks wants to say that nobody needs to go without food," he said. "He ate my handkerchief yesterday, and he tried to eat the clothes pegs out of the basket."

"He's a marvellous goat," said Jerry. "I wish he was mine."

"Perhaps I could give him to you if I can't take him to the Home with me," said Susy-Ann.

"Don't let's talk about that now," said Pip, seeing that Susy-Ann was suddenly looking very gloomy. "What is that noise, Jerry?"

"That? Oh, that's the parrots screeching," said Jerry. "We've got three talking parrots, you know. My word, they're clever! They belong to Madame Clara, and she thinks the world of them!"

Pip suddenly threw his head back and made a noise exactly like the screeching of a parrot. Jerry jumped and stared at him in amazement.

"I say!" he said. "That sounded just like a parrot. How clever of you!"

"Pip can imitate any noise," said Susy-Ann, proudly. "Be a cow, Pip."

Pip at once mooed like a cow. Where he got the deep bellowing noise from, Jerry couldn't think! Two cows in the next field cantered up to the hedge and looked over it. They mooed to Pip.

Pip mooed again and the cows stared in wonder.

"Now do a horse neighing," said Susy-Ann. So Pip neighed and whinnied, and at once there were answering whinnies from the circus horses at the other end of the field.

"It's marvellous!" said Jerry. "I say, Pip, I do wish you could teach *me*."

"I'll try if you like," said Pip. "But I can't teach you much in a few days."

"How did you learn all that?" asked Jerry.

"I didn't learn it," said Pip. "I just found I could do any noise. Listen—what's this?"

He made a chuffing sound—a creaking noise—and a clank!

"A train going into a station and stopping!" shouted Jerry. "Go on—do something else!"

Pip made a curious churring noise, then a honking noise, and then another churring noise.

"That's a motor-car going fast and hooting, and then going slow and stopping!" cried Jerry. "Oh, Pip, you are a real marvel!"

The parrots in the caravan screeched again, and Pip screeched back. A small woman with a very pink face and bright blue eyes came running over to them.

"Jerry! I can hear one of my parrots screeching over here! It must have escaped! Have you seen it?"

"No, Madame Clara," answered Jerry, politely, trying not to laugh. "Have you looked to see if they are all in your caravan?"

"They were when I was there last!" said Madame Clara, and she ran to see. Pip screeched again, and she turned round in astonishment, looking up into the trees and all around.

"Pip! Don't!" begged Jerry, who was nearly bursting with trying not to laugh. "You'll get me into trouble. Madame Clara has a very bad temper."

So Pip did not screech again, and the three children watched Madame Clara go into her caravan to see that all her parrots were there.

She came out again in a minute and called to Jerry. "They're all here! It's very queer—I can't *think* what that noise was!"

"That *was* funny," said Jerry, giggling. "I say, Pip, could you and Susy-Ann come to the show tonight, do you think? My father says he can get you two seats at the back."

"Oh, yes!" cried Pip and Susy-Ann together. "Thank you, Jerry!"

"Well, don't you do any screeching or bellowing or squealing in the show to-night," grinned Jerry. "Or you'll have the people thinking one of our show-animals has escaped and is wandering somewhere among the seats!"

Pip and Susy-Ann were very excited all that day. They had never in their lives seen a circus before. They could hardly wait for the time to come.

But at last it came and the two children went in at the gate with all the other people. Jerry was there to meet them and to tell the man at the gate that they were his friends and need not pay.

He took their arms and ran with them to the big tent. "This is the 'big top'," he said. "That's what we call our show-tent, you know. Look, here are your seats. They are at the back, but you can stand if you want to, and you'll see very well."

"Jerry, do you go into the ring with all the other performers?" asked Susy-Ann.

"No, of course not!" said Jerry. "I'm not much good at anything except feeding animals and doing odd jobs that nobody else wants to do! Well—so long! I'll see you after the show. Hope you enjoy it!"

He disappeared. Pip made a tiny squeaking noise, and his white mouse put her head out from above the little boy's collar.

"I thought Snowball might enjoy seeing the circus too," said Pip to Susy-Ann. "It's a pity you couldn't have brought Mister Binks. I hope you tied him up safely?"

"Well, I tied him up with that piece of wire," said Susy-Ann. "But he may eat it and come."

"Sh!" said Pip. "The circus is beginning!"

There was a sound of trumpets. The children gazed down

at the big red ring in the middle of the great tent. It was spread with sawdust, and was quite empty. The trumpets sounded louder. The great red curtains that hung at one side of the ring, where the entrance was, were suddenly pulled aside.

And in walked or ran or rode all the circus folk! But how different they looked now from the daytime! They no longer wore dirty old jerseys and blouses, caps and shawls, ragged coats and skirts. No—now they were dressed in silks and satins, in glittering silver and gold, in suits and frocks that shone as if they were on fire!

Mr. Phillipino and his daughter Annabella came in first, riding in a golden carriage pulled by four tiny white ponies. Mr. Phillipino jumped out of the carriage when it had gone twice round the ring and stood in the middle cracking his great, whip. In came the beautiful black horses he owned, pawing the ground gracefully, tossing their plumed heads, cantering round and round the ring after the carriage.

Annabella leapt from the carriage, which was taken out by the ponies, and jumped on to one of the black horses. A glittering youth rode another. Then in came the three clowns, turning somersaults and cart-wheels among the horses, shouting and yelling.

Out went the horses, and the clowns ran round on the red plush ring itself, whilst a procession of performers came in—Terry, the sharp-shooter, and his beautiful wife, Juana, the famous sword-swallower, Jinks and Jenks, the wonderful trapeze-folk, Madame Clara and her three parrots sitting on her shoulder, Mr. Hola and his two chimpanzees who walked beside him, fully dressed, holding his hands, Delia and her Dancing Bear, and last of all the three great elephants, Rag, Tag, and Bobtail, with their proud keeper, Mr. Jummy.

They all marched round the ring, whilst Mr. Phillipino

stood in the middle, cracking his whip. Then one by one they all marched out again, and the circus began.

Tan-tan-tara! The trumpets sounded outside once more, and in pranced the beautiful horses again. Annabella and the glittering young man were marvellously clever with them.

"Look at them standing on the horses' backs!" cried Pip in excitement. "Oh, I hope they don't fall!"

But of course they didn't—they not only stood on the horses, they jumped from one to another! They made the horses dance with the music, turning round and round as they danced. It was beautiful to watch.

Then the clowns came in again, and were so funny that the two children almost cried with laughing! They fell over one another, they banged each other with big balloons that burst

with a pop, and they tried to ride a fat old circus horse that was sent cantering into the ring to them.

They all got on to it, and then the fat horse solemnly stood up on its hind legs and let all the three clowns slip off over its tail with a bang-thud-crash! Then the horse picked up one of the clowns by the belt and trotted out of the ring with him, the other two shouting and following.

"Oh, I do love those clowns," said Susy-Ann, in delight. "Look—what's this now, Pip?"

It was the three great elephants who had come to play their game of hockey in the ring. Each elephant held a hockey-stick in his trunk, and when their keeper sent the ball to them, how clever they were at knocking it about from one to the other! There was a small goal set at one side of the ring, guarded by the elephant called Rag, and he didn't let the others score a single goal!

Everyone clapped the clever beasts as loudly as they could when they went out of the ring. The next turn was Juana, the famous sword-swallower. The children watched in astonishment, for his tricks were really amazing.

He swallowed two pocket-knives and a short dagger. It was most astonishing to see them disappear into his mouth and come up again! And then he took a long sword—and, dear me, that went down his surprising throat too, and only the handle was left to be seen!

He flourished the sword in the air as he bowed. Pip couldn't *imagine* how anyone could swallow such a very long weapon!

Then came the two trapeze folk, who climbed a long ladder right up into the roof of the tent till they came to their little swings. And on those swings they did the most daring things! They swung themselves from one swing to another, seeming almost to fly in the air as they went.

Susy-Ann was afraid they might miss the swings and fall, but they never did.

"Anyway, there's a net underneath to catch them if they *do* fall!" said Pip, watching. Jinks hung by his strong teeth from his swing, and Jenks, his partner, was hanging from his by his toes. He suddenly leapt to the other swing, and, as Jinks fell, Jenks caught his upstretched hands and swung him safely across to the swing he had just left. No wonder everybody clapped!

Then in came the clowns again with a ladder, and the times they put it up and tried to climb it and it fell down! Everyone laughed till they could laugh no more. Then Mr. Phillipino cracked his whip again and the clowns ran out. It was Madame Clara's turn.

Her parrots were wonderful. They could say the alphabet, and "Jack and Jill" and "Little Jack Horner".

They sang "Pop goes the Weasel" all together, and made a popping sound at the end. They were really marvellous.

And even more wonderful were Mr. Hola's two amusing chimpanzees, and Delia's Dancing Bear. The chimpanzees could ride bicycles, and work a sewing-machine. Delia's bear wore shoes and did a tap-dance, whilst Delia, in a beautiful glittering frock, danced round too, playing a big concertina.

Terry, the sharp-shooter, was so clever that Susy-Ann and Pip were quite frightened. He put his lovely little wife against a screen, and then shot all round her with his revolver, making a picture of her head, her shoulders, her arms, and her legs! When she stepped away from the screen everyone could see her outline done in bullet-holes!

Then the circus was over. People cheered and clapped and then went out. Half-asleep, Susy-Ann and Pip went too. They tumbled into bed, and dreamt all night long of the wonderful circus. How they wished they belonged to it too!